A THIEF IN FARSHORE

JUSTIN FIKE

THE FARSHORE CHRONICLES, BOOK 1

A Thief In Farshore Copyright © 2019 by Justin Fike.

All rights reserved. Printed in the United States of America. No part of this book may be used or reproduced in any manner whatsoever without written permission except in the case of brief quotations embodied in critical articles or reviews.

This book is a work of fiction. Names, characters, businesses, organizations, places, events and incidents either are the product of the author's imagination or are used fictitiously. Any resemblance to actual persons, living or dead, events, or locales is entirely coincidental.

For information contact www.justinfike.com

Cover design by Janelle Hugel,
www.peregrinecreative.co

First Edition: August 2019

TABLE OF CONTENTS

CHAPTER 1..............................5

CHAPTER 2............................27

CHAPTER 3............................53

CHAPTER 4............................69

CHAPTER 5............................88

CHAPTER 6..........................104

CHAPTER 7..........................121

CHAPTER 8..........................137

CHAPTER 9..........................149

CHAPTER 10........................175

FREE STORY OFFER..................194

THE ADVENTURE CONTINUES......195

For all the misfits, friends, and rogues
who walked this journey with me.

Chapter 1

I'd only been breathing the air of the New World for a few minutes and I already hated it. No rot of open sewage, no horse's sweat, or dust clouds stirred up by ten thousand pairs of feet on market day. Just air so clean and cold it burned the back of your throat, full of salt from the sea and pine sap from the forest just beyond the docks.

"State your name, prisoner."

"It's Charity."

Three months at sea and he hadn't bothered to learn my name. To be fair, I hadn't cared to learn his either, or the names of the other legion soldiers who'd been sent to make sure our chains stayed locked tight during the voyage. Each one looked just like the rest; black hair that had long since outgrown regulation close-crop as days turned to weeks, noses beaked sharper than the bow of our ship, and brown Byzantian skin that had only browned further beneath the fierce sun that beat down on the upper decks each day.

The soldiers had spent the entire trip complaining about the ill fortune that had posted them to a ship sailing to the ass end of the world and taking their bad temper out on those of us chained below decks. The whole journey had been miserable, but the pointless chains they fastened to our ankles every evening had been the worst indignity of all. Where did they think we would escape to, with nothing but rolling sea waves stretching to the horizon in every direction?

He stared at me for a moment, waiting for a family name to go along with my given one, but I had none to add. The Daughters of Vesta had only given me the one when they'd swept me up off the streets, and it was all I'd taken with me again when they'd thrown me out.

"Fair enough, girl."

He marked it down in his ledger, then gestured down the gangplank. I wobbled my way down the length of wood as best my sore and sea-worn legs could manage and turned to look back at the hulk of timber that had been my prison cell for three long months. The *Typhon* was a sturdy, ocean-going vessel. Even a street rat like me could see it was nothing like the sleek galleys which glided through the calm waters of the Mare Nostri back home.

Home. The word still sent a twist through my guts. If you'd asked me back before the magister had sentenced me to slavery and servitude here in their new world, I would have told you that I had no home. Only Byzantia's cobbled streets and twisting alleyways, and the crawlspace above the ovens of the bakery on the Plaza Chrisari in winter. Now that Byzantia and all the other cities of the Imperium were lost to me forever, I found that I'd had enough home to miss after all.

I shuffled down the dock with the other prisoners, linked together as we were by the heavy chain that the ship's crew had retrieved from the stowage hold when we'd first sighted land. The dock led from the deep water where the *Typhon* sat at anchor to a forested shoreline broken by a collection of rough-hewn buildings and dirt tracks that ran along the waterfront. Two of the buildings were large enough to serve as warehouses, and one even had a small canal with a winch dock for punts to pull in and unload cargo, though for now it sat idle. I saw the Consortium's sign hanging over the door of a merchant and lending exchange, a small tavern that was far too quiet for this late hour, and a collection of houses whose walls and beams still bore the white scars and loose splinters of the axe that had planed them.

A few souls had gathered at the end of the docks to stare at the ship, and at us, in undisguised glee. I had no doubt that our arrival was the most exciting event these docks had seen in a long, long time.

"This is Farshore?"

The man chained in front of me kept scanning up and down the coast as though he expected the rest of the city to emerge from the trees at any moment. The despair in his voice would have been comical if I hadn't been feeling the same way myself. I'd known the colony was young, but I'd at least expected something that a country peasant might be tempted to call a town. All I could see above the small collection of rooftops were trees, rocks, and endless sky ahead of us. All I could hear was a looming green silence broken only by the harsh calls of birds I didn't recognize, and the unbroken rumble of the ocean surf at our backs.

"Don't be daft," one of the *Typhon's* sailors snorted as he walked beside us down the dock. "This is just Shoreside. The governor's keen on turning it into a proper port town. Wasn't long ago this was just a dock and a stretch of dry beach. The city lies inland a ways."

A half-dozen soldiers wearing the same legion breastplates and short blades as the one who'd taken my name on the ship waited at the end of the dock. They looked bored, but they unlocked our chains, sorted us into groups, and loaded us into the three wagons that stood waiting with a tired kind of efficiency. The driver snapped his whip, my wagon jolted, and we were off.

"Divines preserve us," whispered the stocky blacksmith on the seat beside me as he made the sign of Jovian's Wise Eye with his shackled hand. His failing business had left him unable to pay his debts, and then in irons aboard a prison ship, which he'd spent the better part of the passage complaining about to anyone who would lend him an ear.

"They've done a shit job of it so far," I said. "Don't see a reason we should expect that to change now."

"Hold your tongue, girl," said the pudgy seamstress seated across from me. I had no idea why she was here, but she hadn't offered her story during the trip, and I hadn't cared to ask. "Or if you must tempt ill fate, at least wait until I'm not seated so close to you."

"Who's to say the gods can even see us from across the waves, or stretch their oh-so-exalted and glorious hands far enough to reach us if they could?" I snapped at her.

"The Divines see all, know all, and are in all."

She spoke the familiar words with reverence, as if they offered the ultimate answer, though they still sounded as hollow as ever to my ears. "We are alive, are we not? What greater sign of their favor do you require?"

I spat over the side of the wagon in answer but decided to waste no more words on her. The passage had taken its toll, true enough. Seven of the forty-one souls who'd begun the trip had perished before we made landfall, but I saw no great Divine hand in my survival. I'd lived because I was too damn stubborn to do otherwise. I had no great hopes for my future here on the ass end of the world, but I'd be damned if I was going to meet my end retching out my guts in the dark, and that was all there was to it.

I rubbed at the chafed and swollen band where the chains had dug into my ankles, and thought about how easy it would be to dive over the side of the wagon and disappear into the tree-line before anyone could stop me. Easy though it might have been, I knew it was just an idle thought, a way to pass the time as our wagon lurched and jolted along the rough dirt trail. I'd heard enough stories about our new home on the passage over that I would have sooner tried my luck at swimming back to Byzantia than brave those woods alone.

The magister who'd sentenced me had expected me to be grateful for his great mercy in sparing me from the headsman's block. As we rode beneath the shadow of trees taller than a temple spire that stretched out their branches like they meant to pluck me from the wagon and devour me, I thought again that it would have been an even greater mercy to just take my head and be done with it. Before Tiberius the Wanderer had made landfall in this accursed place they would have done just that, but the First Colony of the Byzantian Imperium was badly in need of bodies to work her fields and various labors if the mother city wished to continue receiving the wealth it had come to rely on.

When Tiberius' ships had returned with holds filled with riches and word of a new world ripe with fresh opportunities and land for the taking, volunteers had rushed to the docks in the thousands, but the next fleet of ships to return from Farshore brought the whole truth with them, inconceivable though it might have been.

Mythics. Creatures from the ancient legends had swarmed out of the shadows to kill and raid. The sailors spoke of Elves in the forests and Dwarven raiders prowling the seas in great warships, of bestial Orcs roaming the western plains, and feral Halflings who swarmed through the jungles of the south in search of victims for their strange blood rites. Worse monsters still were said to prowl through forests and lurk within caves, ready to pounce on the soft, foolish creatures who had come to their shores so unaware of its dangers.

Every child knew the old stories of brave heroes sent by the Divines to battle the inhuman menace that had once plagued humankind and kept us trembling within our walls at night in the distant past. One of the first lessons Sister Gizella taught me was of the Grand Crusade, when the legions of First Emperor Alexius had swept the last of the mythic creatures into the sea, but I had always assumed that her lessons were no more real than the tales of Chressus and Partho.

Some claimed the sailors' tales were nothing more than sun-addled madness, but the death rolls posted in the marketplace soon had others thinking twice. It wasn't long before the supply of volunteers dried up. It had begun to look like Farshore colony would have to be abandoned, no matter how rich her forests and mines might be, until some genius in the imperial court hit on the idea of sending those convicted of less serious crimes in their stead.

Farshore had already celebrated its sixtieth year by the time I came of age, and the passage of sailing ships leaving Byzantia's docks loaded with prisoners or returning with holds filled with fresh timber, gold and silver ore, furs, and other goods had become a regular occurrence. Now here I sat, rolling along in a wagon like a sow led to slaughter, and trying hard not to jump at every cry and rustle from beyond the forest's edge.

We endured the rest of the ride in silence. Our wagons made poor time, and by my guess the minutes had stretched to nearly an hour. Just as I'd begun to wonder if Farshore colony was as much a drunken sailor's tale as the mythics I'd yet to catch sight of our wagon crested the hill we'd been climbing and broke through the trees to give me my first good look at the city filling the valley below.

It wasn't much to look at. You could have tucked the whole lot of it into Byzantia's east end with room left over. But the sight of straight walls, sloping rooftops, and other evidence of human habitation in this strange and wild land sent a warm comfort through my bones.

Our wagon wound down the dusty road, and as the city grew closer, I saw that even though it was somewhat smaller than I'd expected it was well built. Buildings of wood and stone, some boasting three stories and more, crowded together behind a sturdy wooden wall lined with watch towers. The flag of the Imperium, five golden stars on a field of red, snapped in the breeze atop each of the towers, a defiant spot of color within the endless expanse of muted greens and browns that surrounded it. The sun was beginning to set behind the mountains to the west, and as we wound our way through the valley the glow of lanterns, candles, and tavern fires flickered to life throughout the city.

As we approached the wall, the driver of the lead wagon shouted up at the soldiers standing watch atop the gate, and soon the heavy wooden doors rolled open to allow us to enter. We rumbled through the yawning doorway, and then the gate crashed shut behind me like a portal to the seven hells.

My first sight of Farshore's streets felt oddly familiar. With rooftops and awnings to block the view of the wild lands beyond the walls you could almost believe you rode through any other Byzantian city of moderate size and means. Bakeries and taverns, clothing shops and houses of exchange all lined the streets, with the windows of the homes and apartments above them standing open to let in the fresh air and sunlight. Buckets were thrust out to dump the evening's wash water and stronger waste into the street below. Men and women went about their evening business, most giving our wagon only a brief passing glance. I even spotted a few street urchins and stray dogs, though far fewer of both than I was used to seeing in a city.

But in many ways those similarities only made the differences stand out even stronger. For one thing, the clothing here was a strange sight. It was heavier and more practical than the light, colorful garments that filled Byzantia's streets. The voices that I heard calling to one another from shop windows and across plazas all rang with a strange accent as well. They all spoke Byzantian, but their tones were short and guttural one minute, fluid and musical the next, and I heard a number of unfamiliar words mixed into their speech.

We rode past one shop whose sign I didn't recognize, a rounded glass beaker filled with a bubbling green liquid. I glanced through the door and caught sight of jars filled with eyes, tails, teeth, and worse lining the shelves within, and the strange odor that flooded my nose as we rolled past nearly sent my lunch up into my throat.

Then we took a turn down a new street and things got truly strange.

A smaller wall cut through the city, tracing a straight line from one side of the outer defensive wall to the other to separate one pocket of the city from the rest. Our wagon rumbled past a small gate guarded by two soldiers. The dusk had grown heavier now, but I could still make out shapes moving amongst the streets and buildings beyond the gate, and few of them looked human. Some were no larger than children, but walked alone or in pairs as though they had business to attend to. Some were far, far too large, with hulking shoulders and long, thick legs.

One of those shapes stepped into the light that spilled from a window. Its skin was gray, its black hair was long and matted, and I swear I caught sight of a row of pointed yellow teeth curling up over its lips before our wagon rolled past the gate.

The more I saw of Farshore, the more I realized how far from home I truly was. Finally, our rolling tour came to a stop before the steps of the largest building I had seen yet, the local Temple of the Five Divines. Its twin stone spires soared into the air above me, casting their shadows over the nearby rooftops like the wings of a falcon ready to pounce on its prey. The soldiers ushered us out of the wagons and formed us into two lines at the base of the steps.

"Time to see what new life the Divines have in store for us, eh?" The blacksmith who'd ridden next to me in the cart tried to sound jovial, but fear and tension weighed down his words. The others shuffled their feet, looked up at the buildings around them, and made pointless conversation as they awaited their fate. I kept my mouth shut and my eyes on the ground. They could all accept the hand they'd been dealt without protest if they wished, but not me.

I had a plan. Escape at the first chance I got, then beg, borrow, or steal what I needed to book passage on a ship back to the real world. No matter what it took, no matter how long I had to bide my time, I was going to find my way back home.

***

"Catella Lascari, seamstress, step forward."

As the guard captain called her name, the woman who'd lectured me during our wagon ride walked around the altar to stand before the temple nave, while those of us who remained stood beneath the feet of the statues of the Five Divines that loomed large on the wall behind us.

Farshore's Patriari, the legion officers, nobles, and principle citizens of the colony, walked among us with an uncomfortably keen interest. They'd been drawn by the promise of fresh labor for their various enterprises like city dogs circling a butcher's wagon.

"Thirty-three years of age and convicted of adultery. Sentenced to four years good service.

Notable skills include the sewing and mending of garments."

So much for your lofty piety, madam.

By the way the woman squirmed and kept her eyes fixed on her feet you'd think they'd hauled her out there naked, but holding these proceedings within the temple walls instead of the market square was another one of those mercies the magister had spoken of back in Byzantia. Once our debt was paid, we would become honest citizens once more, and then we might be glad that only two-score others knew of our various sins.

After a short round of bidding, the seamstress was claimed for the barracks by Knight Captain Alexius, a stern-faced man with salt and pepper hair. No doubt his soldiers would thank him for it when they greeted the winter months dressed in new uniforms. Each of those gathered here had been granted a certain degree of credit, determined by their station and the importance of their duties and businesses to the colony, with which to bid for the contracts of the newly arrived convicts.

"Charity of Byzantia, step forward."

I swallowed hard and moved to stand in the space that the seamstress had just vacated. The Five Divines stared down at my back, while Farshore's gentry circled around me, and I couldn't decide which of the two left me more uncomfortable.

"Twenty-one years of age, and convicted of thievery, public drunkenness, resisting of arrest, assault on representatives of the law, licentious and indecent behavior, and blasphemy." I saw more than a few eyebrows raise as my list of crimes rolled on.

It would have saved us some time if you'd just said "convicted of trying to survive."

"Sentenced to ten years good service. No known skills or abilities."

Well, that won't do.

My list of various offenses already did me no favors, but if the good lords and ladies of Farshore colony thought I had nothing to offer, I'd surely be bound for the fields or a mining outpost before the sun had set.

"That's not true! I can read and write."

One of the requirements of continuing to reside with the Daughters of Vesta had been that I attend well to my studies. Their patron was the goddess of wisdom and learning, after all. I'd given them hell for it, of course, but in the end I'd learned what they'd wished to teach me. I'd even come to enjoy those lessons, but if you ever breathe a word of that to Mother Shanti I swear I'll gut you like a carp.

"I'm familiar with history and the classics, and I've a decent head for figures if you don't rush me overmuch."

Even in my wildest dreams I doubted that anyone would risk taking on someone with a history like mine as a clerk or bookkeeper, but there was always a slim chance that one of those present was desperate. Very, very desperate.

"A lady thief who reads Porathus and Scytho? Now I have seen everything."

The gathering chuckled at the joke as a man walked up to give me a more thorough inspection. He was several inches taller than me, heavy set but not exactly fat, and kept his hair and beard well-trimmed to match his fine clothes.

"Governor Caligus," the guard captain said as he saluted.

So, this is the man himself.

I'd heard of the governor back in Byzantia even before I got nicked. The emperor had sent him to take command of Farshore after the previous governor died of a fever, and he'd done enough to improve the colony's fortunes and reputation in that time to lead some of the Imperium's more optimistic citizens to volunteer for the ocean crossing once more. I gritted my teeth and offered him a proper curtsy as he circled around behind me.

"It seems a shame to waste such a delicate young creature on hard labor. Perhaps we can find a better use for your many talents, eh?"

He came to a stop in front of me once again with a smile on his face and a light in his eye that was anything but fatherly.

Oh shit.

I've never held to any pretense of beauty. My jaw is too square and my hands too rough. I crop my soot-black hair with a dull knife when it's grown too long, and the one time I got my hands on a box of rouge and blush I sold it to the first corner doxy I could find for a pouch of coppers and a decent meal.

But although I wasn't born beautiful, neither was I blessed with enough ugliness to keep men's eyes away from me completely. I have legs, breasts, and breath in my lungs, and I've found that for most men that's more than enough to attract their unwanted attentions.

"What say you, girl? Wouldn't you like to come work for me? I assure you that employment in my household comes with all manner of…benefits."

I knew how this worked. Now that he'd shown interest none of the others would dare to bid for me even if they'd wanted to. I felt a cold chill crawl its way up my spine, but I gave him my best smile to show him that I still had all my teeth. He leaned forward for a closer look.

As soon as he'd come close enough, I drove my knee between his legs as hard as I could.

I may be many things, but I'm nobody's whore.

The governor collapsed to his knees, clutching his privates and gasping for air as the gathered gentry erupted in a mixture of startled gasps and hearty laughter.

"Come near me again and I'll take your bits clean off, you shit eating bastard."

I went for his face, but the guard captain caught my wrists and pinned my arms behind my back.

"Aaaaaagh!" The governor finally found his voice, sounding for all the world like a zitar with its strings stretched to breaking. I knew I was about to pay for my moment of defiance, but I would rather endure a whole lifetime of digging in a mine than ten years as a bed slave. "Take this demon to the arena pits!"

Double shit. I didn't think of that.

Despite Farshore's strangeness, it seemed that a fondness for arena games was one of the few legacies of the old world that had survived the time and distance intact. In Byzantia the crowds loved few things more than a contest of arms to honor the Divines, especially one that ended in blood.

I was rather partial to the arena myself. Its crowded stands had always proved a ready source of unguarded pockets to pick, but the thought of being the one to stand out there on the arena sand while the crowd screamed for my death drained all the strength from my legs.

CHAPTER 2

The guard captain passed me off to two soldiers who'd been standing watch at the temple door and ordered them to hand me over to the Master of the Games without delay. We set off at a brisk pace, each one with a hand clasped tight to one of my elbows. Neither man seemed inclined to conversation, which suited me just fine. My head was still reeling from the speed of the day. I'd awoken this morning in the same corner of the prison ship that I'd slept in every night for the past three months, and now I was being marched to my eventual but certain death before the sun had finished its dive behind the city walls.

It seemed that my sour luck had managed to follow me across the waves. I thought briefly of the seamstress' warning against tempting the Divines' ire. It hardly seemed fair that the gods, who as far as I could tell had never lifted a finger in my aid or defense, should be so quick to condemn me for speaking my mind. But now that I considered it, that seemed like exactly the sort of petty horse shit they would find entertaining.

In truth, I remember little of that forced march through Farshore's streets. I recall faces turned towards me, a good deal of pointing and whispered words, but little else. At one point we wove through a series of market stalls whose vendors had begun packing away their goods for the evening. Sometime later we marched through the pools of light that spilled out the door of a tavern ringing with voices, laughter, and the clatter of plates and mugs on wooden tables. I'm not sure how long our trek lasted, only that the fog that clouded my thoughts abruptly cleared as our journey through the streets came to a stop before the arena's walls.

Farshore's arena was nowhere near as grand as Byzantia's Hippodrome, but it still towered over me as I craned my neck to look up at the imposing bulk of its high wall crowned with the fiery glow of the sunset beyond it. The arena curved outward, molding the street that ran in front of it into a half circle. From the wooden guard tower that rose up behind it I guessed that the structure had been built up against the city wall itself. The entrance was a wide archway designed to let the crowds pour in all at once, and I could see the open arena floor and rows of benches within.

The guards ignored the entrance, however, and led me around the wall to the left until we stood facing a smaller, iron-banded door watched over by a large, muscular man in a loose shirt and pants. He sported a black mustache whose tips draped down to frame his mouth and swayed in the breeze as leaned his chair back against the arena walls. I spotted a wicked-looking cudgel set with iron bands leaning against the wall next to him.

At first I thought he was napping on the job, but he cracked one eye open as we approached. As we came to a stop in front of him the man yawned, then let his chair fall forward to sit upright once again as he stared up at my two traveling companions with obvious boredom.

"Got a prisoner for the pits," said Left Guard.

"Get gone," said the man, his words rolling out in the lilting accent of the Gaellean tribes from the forests north of Byzantia.

"This is the arena, not a boarding house for children."

"Governor gave the order himself, so shut it and take her to the Master," said Right Guard. He gave me a little shove forward to emphasize his point.

The man sighed and stood to his feet. He was a full head taller than all three of us, and I had to fight the urge to take a step backward as he looked down at me.

"You came in on the prison ship this afternoon?"

I nodded.

"And you couldn't manage a single night without getting yourself sentenced to the arena?"

"I'm good at making friends."

I was surprised to see him smile in return, and I realized that he was younger than I'd first thought. A few years older than me at most.

"I can see that." He turned and lifted the heavy iron bar from the door with one hand, then pushed it open. A set of stairs led down into darkness, lit only by a torch that stood in a wall sconce just inside the door. Left Guard shoved me forward again, then turned and marched off with Right Guard close on his heels.

I scanned the street, judging the distance between me and the closest building. It wasn't far, but to reach shelter I'd have to get past the Mustache Giant, and my instinct told me that for all his size the man could move quick when he wanted to. Besides, where would I go? Unlike Byzantia, I had no bolt holes or hideaways to lay low in. No, for now the safest way for me was forward, which was a rather depressing thought considering that "forward" meant "down into the arena pit where men wait their turn to fight to the death." I sighed, took one last look at the rays of the sun spread across the open sky, then stepped through the door.

Mustache Giant followed me in and pulled the door shut with a thud behind him as he retrieved the torch and gestured for me to lead the way. Didn't want me at his back, even if I was only half his size, which meant that he was taking me at least a little bit seriously. I decided that I liked him.

"You got a name, Mustache?"

We walked down a dozen steps in silence, until I thought he wasn't going to answer.

"Cael," his voice rumbled at my back and bounced off the walls.

"I'm Charity."

We reached the bottom of the staircase to find another heavy wooden door waiting for us. Cael reached around me and used a key I hadn't spotted before to unlock it, then slipped the key inside his shirt. He caught my eyes following it, and grinned.

"Somehow, I doubt that." He pulled the door open, gesturing again for me to step through first.

I found myself standing in a hallway of carved stone. The floor was level, and the ceiling was short enough that Cael had to tilt his head just a bit to avoid bumping into it, but it was dry, and more torches lined both walls to fill the space with light. There was a door set into the wall just a few paces ahead on our right. Cael led me up to it and knocked twice.

"Enter," called a thin voice from inside. Cael opened the door and we both stepped through.

The room turned out to be an office, not richly furnished, but comfortable. Shelves loaded with books and scrolls lined one wall, a tapestry of green fabric with beautiful, spiraling patterns in silver thread hung on the other, and a large desk stood between them. A table stood in the corner covered with bottles filled with strange colored liquids, half-burnt candles and various stones, leaves, animal bones, and bowls of powder. Lanterns gave the room a brighter light than the hallway outside, and a fireplace was dug into the back wall. It held a few burning logs which cracked and sizzled as they fought to keep the underground room warm, and a man sat at the desk with his back to the fire. He looked up as we entered, and frowned.

"What's this, then?"

"A new prisoner for the games," Cael answered. "Sent by the governor himself, I'm told."

The man's frown deepened, but he stood and circled around the desk. He was as noticeably short as Cael was noticeably tall, with a thin face, beaked nose, and thinning black hair. He regarded me with a long, appraising look before he spoke, looking for all the world like an ill-fed bird in winter.

"I am Trebonious Leucator, Master of the Games here in the arena, and now the right hand of the Divines themselves as far as you're concerned."

I considered making a comment about exactly what he could do with his right hand, but even I have my limits of unnecessary stupidity. Instead I just nodded and waited for him to continue.

"This is your world now. You live for the crowds, and will most likely die for them."

He tilted his head to one side and studied me as though he sought to fix the exact worth of my life in coin and found the answer somewhat disappointing.

"Fight well, and you will enjoy glory and some measure of comfort, perhaps even freedom and riches. Fight poorly, and, well…," he shrugged.

"But most important of all is this: do not cause trouble, attempt to escape, or inconvenience me in any way. If you're smart, this conversation is the last that we shall have together. If you force me to turn my attention to you again you will find me far less pleasant. Am I understood?"

I nodded again. I could already tell that this Trebonious did not suffer from an abundance of good humor, and with the way this day was going I thought it best not to trust my mouth overmuch.

"Excellent. Now, while I assure you that I take you and all the other criminal garbage who wash ashore here entirely at your word, common sense dictates that I not rely solely on your good intentions to ensure your behavior."

He turned and walked to the table covered in strange items, then retrieved a wooden box and began unpacking its contents. He placed a small pair of silver scissors, a spool of silver thread, and a knife with a blade of clear glass side by side on his desk.

"Now, hold still."

He picked up the scissors and stepped towards me. I don't know about you, but I have never in my life known a time when someone ordering me to hold still and then advancing on me with a sharp object worked out in my favor. I tried to jump back, but instead of opening some distance between us all I managed to do was collide with six plus feet of muscle and mustache. Cael had moved to stand behind me while I was distracted.

"Relax," he said, although he had a pretty firm grip on my arms as he said it. "He's not going to hurt you."

If the man wasn't so damnably tall I might have tried putting my heel in his groin and telling him to relax, but I wasn't sure I could reach high enough to do any real damage, and I didn't see much sense in angering him without getting results. As I was thinking all that through Trebonious stepped forward and snipped off a good-sized lock of my hair.

"That's it?" I asked, feeling equal parts confused and relieved.

"Almost." He grabbed my hand in a surprisingly strong grip for a man his size and made a quick, shallow cut across my palm with the glass knife. He muttered some strange words under his breath, then smeared the ends of the lock of hair in the blood that had welled up from the cut.

"There, now I have what I need."

He returned to the desk and began to wrap the silver thread around the lock of hair.

"Having just arrived from Byzantia I'm sure you are filled with all manner of skepticism regarding the magical arts, but I have neither the time nor the inclination to attempt to change your mind. I will say this only once, and I advise you to suspend your disbelief if you would prefer for your insides to remain on the inside."

He held the loop of hair in front of my face. A single drop of my blood clung to the bottom for a moment, then plunged to the floor. Just looking at the thing set my teeth on edge.

"When I finish the incantation this evening, this will become an effigy. Your effigy, specifically. I'll spare you the technical details and simply say that with this I can bring you to such a gruesomely painful end that being eviscerated in the arena would seem a mercy in comparison. I trust you will not force me to use it?"

"Not planning on it, no."

I kept my voice and expression neutral. He clearly believed in what he said even if I didn't. The gullible and foolish wasted many an evening back home with whispered talk of strange forces and magic spells that could charm a lover, curse an enemy, or worse. Those rumors had grown a hundred-fold since the first ships returned from Farshore carrying word of terrible monsters and mythical races who wielded strange magics, but so far I'd seen no sign of any such thing. Whatever I'd seen through the gate we'd ridden past earlier had probably just been a trick of the dim light and an anxious mind.

In fact, I was beginning to suspect that all the talk of wild magic and wizards had been nothing more than eager imagination and exaggerated reports spun by sailors looking to impress their friends into buying them drinks. The clerics of the Divines made dire proclamations every day about the ill fortune that would befall those who defied the will of the gods, but little ever came of it. Was this really any different?

But, magic or no, this man had the power to make my life miserable, short, or both, so I thought it best to avoid offending another powerful official in the city unless I absolutely had to. The only thing I wanted now was to get out of his sight and hope he forgot all about me by dinner time.

"Good. Cael, show her the facilities and see her settled in her quarters." Trebonious turned back to his desk in dismissal as Cael lead me back out into the hallway and shut the door behind him.

We continued down the hall for several paces in silence.

"Kitchens," Cael said as we passed by a door. "And the guard barracks," he said with a nod towards another door further down.

"Not that it matters. You won't be passing by this way again."

His voice remained light and pleasant, but the complete certainty with which he spoke those words did more to dampen my spirits than any of Trebonious' threats had managed.

Soon the hallway ended in another heavy door with an iron crossbar that slid into the stone of the wall itself. I heard a muted hum of voices on the far side, which rose to a full-pitched roar as Cael drew back the crossbar and pushed the door open.

The room beyond was far larger and wider than any I had seen thus far. Oil lamps hung from a ceiling that was twice the height of the hallway, and the floor was set with a dozen long tables that currently hosted an evening meal in full swing. More than fifty men of all sizes and colors sat on benches or stood against the walls as they ate, and their shouts, curses, and laughter echoed through the hall. I counted six guards with swords at their hips and cudgels like Cael's in their hands, but they seemed content to leave the men to their meal as long as no one was causing trouble.

My look around the room ended on the table nearest me. Two men sat on one side, cheering for a third. Their champion was nearly a match for Cael in size, and was locked in the middle of an arm-wrestling contest with a fellow who sat across the table. He was as thick as an ale barrel, with arms and legs like fallen logs, and was short enough that he had to kneel on the bench to get good leverage on the table. His head was crowned with a shock of fiery red hair that flowed down into one of the most impressive beards I had ever seen. His opponent strained and heaved at his arm so hard that his face had turned red, but the short man mostly just looked bored.

Finally, the bearded one seemed to tire of their game. He slammed the other man's hand down on the table as if he was swatting a fly, then jumped up onto the table and spread his arms wide.

"Ha! This be no sport at all! Are there none here fit to challenge Magnus Ironprow?" He leaned down, snatched up the man's mug, and drained its contents in three large gulps.

"Who be next to donate their beer to a more worthy stomach?"

The rest of the room mostly ignored his taunts and jeers, but I couldn't pull my eyes away from him. He looked like no man I'd ever seen before. In fact, I was starting to realize that he didn't look much like a man at all.

"Is..is that a…?" I seemed to have trouble forming words.

"The dwarf? What of him?"

Cael sounded like I'd just asked him why the sky was blue. I hadn't really known what to make of the strange tales of mythic races in the new world, but I certainly had never expected to see one standing on top of a table shouting for another round of arm wrestling.

"You have a mythic in here?"

"Oh right, I forgot that you just arrived. We've more than one, actually."

Cael pointed to another table, where a slender man with flowing blonde hair was playing at cards with a half dozen others. I'd overlooked him before, but now that Cael pointed him out I noticed that his features were far more delicate and graceful than any human face I'd seen before, and I spotted two pointed ear tips peeking through his hair.

"Elf." Cael shifted his hand to point towards the shadows in the far corner of the room.

At first glance I thought he pointed at thin air. Then a pair of yellow eyes flashed in the lamplight, and I realized that the shadows concealed someone even smaller than the dwarf. The eyes shifted back and forth, constantly scanning the room. As they swung back again, they fixed on mine with the sudden attention of a hunting bird. As the figure leaned forward into the light I realized that it was a small woman, with a heart-shaped face beneath brown hair that had been braided in long, tight rows across her scalp to hang down her back.

"Halfling. Wouldn't recommend trying to make friends."

The halfling clearly knew we were speaking of her. She grinned at me like a cat sighting prey, and ran the tip of her tongue across her small, white teeth.

Cael's finger moved towards another table, where a hulking brute with wiry black hair sat scooping great spoonfuls of stew into its mouth. I saw now that its skin was more of a grey-green than the black I had mistaken it for in the lamp light, and that the mouth making short work of the food was lined with round, pointed teeth.

"What is that?" I whispered.

"*She* is an orc. Nataka."

My face must have gone a bit pale, because when Cael turned back towards me he burst into a fit of laughter.

"Cuernos' balls, girl, she's not going to eat you. Not unless you give her a reason to. Although I might suggest a bit less staring."

I realized my jaw had dropped open a bit, so I shut it and fixed my eyes on Cael's smiling and very human face.

"But what are they doing here?"

Cael just shrugged.

"Pissed off the wrong person or broke the law in the city, same as you. Magnus broke every table in a tavern on the Breezeway during a brawl, Nataka beat three men senseless for offending the spirits or some such, and we found Sheska chewing her way through a merchant's ribcage."

I glanced up to see if he was having one over on me. He wasn't smiling.

"Claims he earned his death. From what I knew of the merchant she may have been right. Now the elf just walked up and knocked on the door one day asking if he could join the arena. Strangest damn thing I've ever seen, but his kind is always strange. It's more mythics than we usually have at one time, I suppose, but that just means bigger crowds."

"Won't their kin come for them? You know, be angry that we've thrown them in here to fight or die?"

"Mmm, those that visit Farshore or choose to take up residence here are told of our laws and what comes of breaking them. If anything, their folk think we're a bit soft. A chance to fight your way to freedom is a damned sight better than most of them would give a criminal. Come on, let's get you settled."

Cael led me down the center aisle that ran between the tables towards an open doorway on the far wall. I felt the eyes of everyone in the room turn towards and the raised voices fade into whispers and muttered speculation as we walked. He led me to an empty table at the far end of the room and gestured towards the bench.

"Have a seat. The guards will bring you food, and you're granted one half-mug of beer with each meal."

"You don't get many women here, I take it?"

Cael turned around, and the volume of noise returned to normal as he glared about the room before turning back to me.

"Not many, no. Not human ones, anyways. You might stand out a bit until they get used to you, but you don't need to worry about anyone bothering you. Stay within sight of a guard and you'll be safer than if you went walking the streets alone."

Great. Inhuman monsters straight out of a bedtime story, but I'm the strange one in the room?

"Go ahead and eat," Cael continued. "I need to speak to the quartermaster about your room. I'll be back." He turned and left without waiting for a reply.

I kept my head down until a guard passed by and left a bowl of stew and a mug of beer on the table. I tucked in, and was surprised to find that the food was actually pretty good. Nothing fancy, but better than a lot of meals I'd eaten back home, and a damn sight better than the ship's biscuits and water they'd fed us during the crossing. Being sentenced to the arena was basically a death sentence, but at least I'd eat well while I waited for the end.

A shadow fell across my table, and I looked up to find a pure-bred Byzantian alley bruiser blocking my lamplight. His hair was shaved down to his scalp and his nose had been broken at least once before, but it was his eyes that gave him away. They were the eyes of a man who'd grown used to taking what he wanted whenever he damn well pleased.

"You're in my seat," he growled.

I'd seen his type a thousand times. They were common as paving stones in my part of town, and suddenly I felt right at home. Mythical creatures on the far side of the world were one thing, but this was a good old-fashioned shake down, and that was something I understood. I hadn't expected the testing to start quite so soon, but if this thug and his friends were that eager to find out where I was going to stand around here, who was I to say no? Even as adrenaline flooded through my veins I couldn't help but smile.

"Thanks," I said, keeping his attention on my face while my hand inched towards my mug. "It's been a hell of a day. I think I needed this."

"Don't thank me yet, puppet. We haven't discussed how you'll be making it up to me."

"Well, how bout we start with a drink?"

I flung my mug at his head before he could answer. I hated to waste good beer, but the opening it bought me was well worth it. I screamed and launched myself at him, ramming my knee into his gut with all the force I could manage, then smashing my soup bowl over his head as he doubled over. He dropped to all fours as the clay bowl shattered and sent hot soup into his eyes. I'd hoped the blow would put him down for keeps, but he just shook his head, sending beer foam and cooked vegetables flying in all directions. He fixed me with a look of pure murder and started to launch himself at me.

A knee struck his back and drove him to the floor with a thud, and an iron-banded cudgel smacked the stone an inch from his nose.

"Saying hello to the new blood, Borus?" Cael asked.

For a minute I thought Borus would try to fight back. Then he seemed to think better of it.

"Aye," he growled, "I was just offering a friendly greeting when this *bruta* jumped me."

"Hmm. I'll tell the guard to keep you safe from her from now on."

Laughter echoed through the room, and Borus flushed red all across his shaved head. Cael looked up at me.

"I take it you've finished your meal?"

"Quite, and I enjoyed every minute of it."

Cael just shook his head and pointed me towards the open doorway that I assumed led back to the fighters' rooms.

"Let's get you settled, then." He took my arm and marched me out of the mess hall without another word.

The corridor we entered branched to the left and right, and the walls of both passages were lined with narrow wooden doors set into the stone wall. We turned left and walked for a while in silence. I could tell that he was upset, but I figured if he was bothered enough to say something then he'd speak up, and if he wasn't then there was no need for me to do it for him.

"I guess you really are good at making friends," he finally said into the silence.

"I was only defending myself," I protested. "If I'd backed down the first time some two-copper thug bared his teeth at me, everyone else would know I was easy pickings."

"But that wasn't just some two-copper thug. Borus is the arena champion."

Cael might as well have just dumped a bucket of ice-cold water over my head.

"What?"

"Going on four years now, the longest anyone I know of has held the title. He's won so many bouts that we've stopped counting. Trebonious granted him his freedom last year, believe it or not. Borus told him the arena was his home now, and he had no intention of ever leaving."

And some twig of a girl just broke a soup bowl over his head in front of all his friends. Wonderful.

We came to a stop in front of one of the last doors on the wall before the hallway ended in another heavy, locked door. Cael pushed it open to reveal a simple, bare room. Four stone were walls lit by a small lantern. A straw pallet, a chamber pot, and a stool were all that waited for me inside.

"This is mine?"

"It's not much, but the door locks from the inside, and you can't beat the view."

"It's perfect," I said, and I meant it. A room of my own. It was nicer than anything I'd seen since the

Daughters of Vesta had tossed me out and closed the temple doors behind me.

"So what happens now? Do I have to report for inspection or something?"

"Ha, no, nothing like that. In fact, you're free to mind your own business during the day unless there's a fight scheduled."

"When's the next one?"

"Tomorrow," he answered, then chuckled at my involuntary gasp. "Don't worry, I'm sure the Master won't send you out onto the sand that fast. And don't worry about Borus, either. Just keep your head down for a few days. Another win in the arena should do wonders for his pride, and he'll forget all about you."

"I'll try."

He nodded, and turned to leave.

"And Cael?" He stopped and looked back at me.

"Thank you."

He seemed surprised at first, then a pleased grin spread across his face. He nodded, then walked back down the corridor.

I stepped inside my new home and closed the door. I drew the bolt home, paused for a minute, then checked again to make sure it was as locked as it could get. I wasn't sure what time it was, but with no way to see the sun I supposed it didn't really matter, and I was exhausted. I blew out the lantern, stretched out on the pallet, and fell asleep before I'd finished my third breath.

CHAPTER 3

I woke up to the sound of muffled voices in the hallway outside my door. I still had no sense of what time it was, but after smashing the better part of my last meal over Borus' head I was hungry enough that I didn't much care. As I opened the door and stepped into the hall the two bruisers who'd been chatting it up a few cells down caught sight of me and went quiet. They stared at me as I walked past, but didn't make a move or speak to me. Apparently word of my run in with the arena champion had already made the rounds.

First day here and I'm already famous. Lucky me.

The common room was mostly empty when I wandered in. A few men sat alone or in pairs around the room, and I spotted the blonde elf-man cleaning off his plate at a nearby table.

I felt their eyes follow me as I moved to sit at the same table that Borus had tried to roust me from yesterday. I glared around the room, daring someone to say something about it, but they all just turned back to their meals as the quiet hum of morning conversation picked back up again.

A few minutes later a guard set a bowl of porridge and hunk of dark bread in front of me. I tucked in and tried to think of some way to keep myself alive and un-maimed through the end of the week.

I'd never been to prison before, but I'd talked to enough of those who had to understand the way of it well enough. I'd made the biggest man here look stupid, so it was sure as shit he was looking to make an example of me to keep others from trying to do the same. Now every man here who wanted to be on better terms with him had a good reason to rough me up, or worse, and it didn't take a Vestan Sister to deduce how long that list would be.

Someone would get to me sooner or later. It wasn't a happy thought, but trying to fool myself into thinking otherwise wouldn't change the facts, which meant my only hope of keeping my skin in one piece was either to make nice with Borus somehow, or find enough folks willing to watch my back to make the risk of trying something too high. Either way, that meant making friends, and making friends fell just above growing daisies out of my ass on the list of things that I was good at.

I couldn't help but let out a sigh as I chewed my breakfast. How did I keep managing to turn a bad thing worse? First the senator whose purse I'd snatched by mistake back in Byzantia to get myself sentenced to this shithole in the first place, then the governor and Borus once I'd arrived. After years of doing a reasonably good job of keeping my head down and my stomach filled, it seemed I'd suddenly developed a stunning capacity for pissing off exactly the wrong person at exactly the wrong time.

Still, thinking back over the chain of events that had led me here, I couldn't honestly say I'd do things any different if I was given the chance.

Nothing about life is fair. Never has been, and never will be. The strong and the rich hold all the cards, and they know exactly how to play them. The only thing a street rat like me has going is that they don't ever expect you to fight back, so when life backs you into a corner your only play is to hit first as hard as you can and hope it buys you enough time to run. It had worked for me well enough so far, but somehow I didn't think that either fighting or running were going to save me now.

"I'd offer you a copper for your thoughts, but from the look on your face I'm not sure they'd be worth the coin."

I looked up and found the elf man standing over me with a smile on his face. It took me a moment to realize that the words I'd heard had been his.

"You can talk?"

Surprise had loosened my tongue, and those words were the first that tumbled out.

So much for making friends, but the smile on his face just spread into a grin.

"I should certainly hope so, or else my dear parents would be even more disappointed in me than they already are."

I felt the blood rising to my cheeks as I shook my head. He might be an inhuman monster, but he wasn't half bad to look at, and here I was babbling like a sun-addled idiot.

"I just didn't expect you to speak Byzantian, is all. Don't your people have their own language?"

"Indeed we do, but I've taken a liking to yours."

He sat down on the opposite bench without waiting for an invitation.

"It's so colorful. I don't know how you'd begin to call someone a shit eating cock-for-brains in elvish, but I'm certain it wouldn't have half the same spice. Besides, your Byzantian is a rather simple tongue to master, truth be told. Nothing like trying to get your mouth around a dwarven syllable, that's for certain. I suppose that's why many here in Danan have adopted your speech as a sort of common language. Makes it a far sight easier to communicate, given that most would rather chop off their own hand than be heard speaking their enemies' native tongue. So, thank you for that I suppose."

"Danan? I thought this city was called Farshore?"

"Your city is, but I'm speaking of the continent you built it on, love. Goodness, haven't they even bothered to tell you its name? Oh, and speaking of names, mine is Alleron. At your service, to be sure."

"Charity," I mumbled as I shoveled the last of the porridge into my mouth. It didn't seem like this Alleron planned anything that might force me to break my bowl over his head, but I wanted to get all the food out of it this time, just in case.

"So I've heard. In fact, I'd wager there's not a man in here who hasn't. You made quite an entrance."

"That bad, huh? Does Borus have a lot of friends?"

"Lanari's tits, I should think not. He's a shit eating cock-for-brains."

He paused, and his eyes drifted towards the ceiling as though they chased after some important thought that had nearly escaped him.

"On the other hand, I've never before seen an individual who was quite so adept at killing people, so most go out of their way to remain in his good graces. It did my heart a world of good to see you go after him the way you did."

"Glad I could brighten your day."

I'm normally fairly good at reading people. You have to be to stay alive on the streets, but I had no idea what to make of this one. His smile was friendly enough, but something about the grace in his movements or the way he kept a casual watch on the room told me that he could take care of himself if he needed to.

"So, Alleron, what are you doing down here in the pits, anyway? Did you eat someone you weren't supposed to?"

Most of the Farshore stories I'd heard either started or ended with someone being eaten by a mythic, but my question mostly just seemed to confuse him.

"I volunteered, actually."

"You can do that?"

"I wasn't entirely certain myself until I tried, but that Trebonious fellow seemed happy enough to have a 'sharp ear' in his arena when I asked him about it."

"But why would you want to risk your life down here by choice? You get tired of breathing?"

"Nothing of the sort. In fact, I'm waiting to meet someone here."

"Oh? Friend of yours?"

"Not yet, but I'm hoping she will be one day."

"Wait, then how do you know the person you're waiting for will end up here if you haven't met them yet?"

He leaned forward as though he wanted to swap secrets, so I leaned forward too.

"I have *foreseen* it."

His voice was full of cheap theatrics, and he wiggled his fingers in front of his face as though he were playing with invisible puppets. He grinned and raised one eyebrow as he waited for me to laugh at his joke. The only problem being that I had no bleeding idea what he was going on about. All I could do was stare back at him in confusion as his smile wilted away.

"Um, you know…magic, that is."

Just then I was glad that I'd already finished my food. I'm sure I would have choked on it otherwise.

"Say what now?"

Alleron laughed and shook his head.

"Ah yes, you're fresh off that boat of yours. Are there truly no wizards or sorceresses where you come from? Not even a hedge witch or two? Life must be exceedingly dull there."

I only half heard what he said after that. A good night's sleep had put Trebonious' threatening talk of magic out of my mind. At the time I'd dismissed it as nothing more than the eccentric ramblings of a man who'd been away from Byzantia a little too long; just one more strange part of a strange day. Yet now an elf (and I had only just begun to make my peace with using that word as it was) sat across the table from me, prattling on about magic like we were discussing suits of clothing or possible breakfast options.

"...not as flashy as Evocation magic of course, though I dare say it's a damned sight more practical indoors. Most laugh when they hear that I've devoted the better part of the past century to mastering the nuances of Divination, but I wouldn't trade it for all the stone golems or pillars of balefire in the Emerald Magus' spell tome."

I knew that some of the Divines' clerics had shoved the stick of holy righteousness so far up their asses that they'd been able to channel the gods' power into miraculous signs and wonders, but none would ever have been mad enough to claim that the power was their own. The old legends were filled with enchantments; fire from the sky, hundred year sleeps, conjured beasts and the like, but everyone knew they were just stories.

Yesterday I'd have sooner believed a man offering to sell me a gilded mansion in the Silk District on the cheap than one claiming to weave spells and incantations, but I was having a harder and harder time ignoring the fact that everyone around here seemed to take the idea as a given. I realized that Alleron had paused and seemed to be waiting to hear my thoughts on the matter.

"Well…good for you, I suppose. Most people are idiots anyway."

His face brightened.

"And here I thought I was the only one who'd noticed that. Come on, Trebonious will be posting the matches for today's games any minute now. Care to join me in a round of pointing and laughing at the unlucky sods who'll be risking life and limb today?"

In truth I didn't much care who would be fighting in the games now that I knew my name wouldn't be on the list. Alleron seemed eager to go, however, and as I'd somehow managed to avoid offending him so far, I decided to at least make some effort to keep it that way. I nodded, grabbed the last of the bread off my plate, and stood to follow him.

Alleron threaded between tables as he headed toward the door on what I had come to think of as the west wall. A guard stood next to it, cudgel in hand and a scowl on his face, but he made no move to stop us as Alleron reached forward and swung the door open, so I followed him into the hallway. It was a short corridor of blank stone that ended in another door. I could hear the muted sound of a crowd of voices through its thick wooden planks, and when Alleron opened it and stepped through I saw that most of those who'd been gathered in the common room when I arrived now milled around the room inside.

The first thing I noticed about the large room was the glorious morning sunlight that flooded into it through the open grates in the ceiling. The sudden brilliance sent a shock of pain through my eyes, but I drank it in all the same. Even though I'd only spent a day or so underground, I was surprised at how much a spot of real sunlight did to lift my spirits.

As my eyes adjusted, I scanned the rest of the large, circular room and realized that it was mostly devoted to training and general exercise. Boulders of various sizes were lined up against the far wall just waiting for the next muscle ox to lift or roll them about. They stood next to racks filled with wooden or blunted practice weapons, while battered straw dummies and sand pits for wrestling or sparring were spread around the room.

None of the men around us were training, however. They stood alone or in small groups, filling the room with the hum of conversation. I scanned their faces and let out a small sigh of relief when I saw that Borus was not among them. Still, I knew better than to let down my guard. Just because the big dog wasn't here didn't mean another one of his pack wouldn't try to take a swipe at me if I gave them the chance. I caught sight of the orc Cael had called

Nataka exchanging quiet words with a large bearded man and the dwarf Magnus on the far side of the room, but I saw no sign of the halfling.

No one paid either Alleron or myself much notice as we entered. Probably because they all kept one eye on the only other door I could see. Its heavy frame, iron bands, and lack of a handle all told me that it led out to the guards' quarters and offices I'd passed through on my way in yesterday.

Then the room echoed with the rasp of an iron bar being drawn back and the squeak of protesting hinges as the door swung open to reveal Cael's tall form standing on the other side. The shadow of a smile that had played at the corners of his mouth yesterday was nowhere to be seen. In fact, if I didn't know better, it looked to me like he wanted to hit someone, and he didn't much care who it was.

He walked into the room without acknowledging anyone. I noticed that he carried a sheet of paper in one hand and a small hammer and spike in the other. He crossed to the large wooden column that supported the ceiling in the center of the room, pressed the paper to it, and drove the spike into it with one solid strike of the hammer.

Everyone crowded forward to get a look at the page he had nailed to the column as Cael turned and marched back the way he had come. I kept my eyes on Cael's back as he shoved his way to the door. He seemed in a hurry to leave, but he paused as he reached the door to look back over the crowd. I was surprised when his gaze found mine and stopped there. He stared at me for a moment, his face so still and cold that I couldn't begin to guess at what he was thinking. Then he frowned, shook his head, and turned to leave, drawing the heavy door closed behind him with a crash. The look on his face as he'd turned away left a cold, queasy feeling in the pit of my stomach. It was the kind of look a man wears to a friend's funeral.

The crowd was pressed in tight around the column, but one by one they pushed their way free and headed out of the room after they'd had their chance to look at the page, so Alleron and I just waited at the back for things to thin out a bit. I noticed that more than a few of those who left cast glances of their own in my direction as they passed by. None of them were friendly.

"Nervous?" Alleron asked as a little half-smile tugged at the corners of his mouth.

"Of course not," I lied. "Are you?"

"Hardly. I won my last match, after all. There's no reason for you to worry, either. Trebonious always gives winners and new blood alike a break from the games to get their feet back under them."

That might have made me feel better if I'd had a chance to take it in, but Alleron spotted a gap in the crowd and dove into it, pulling me along behind him. After a short scuffle he managed to force his way to the front and stopped to read the page, blocking my view with a curtain of golden hair.

"Oh my…well, this is unexpected."

"Damn it, Alleron. Let me through!"

I managed to elbow him aside far enough to get a look at the page. As I'd expected, it was a list of names paired together; the schedule of who would be facing off against each other in today's games. I scanned the list, picking my way through a lot of names I didn't recognize until I found one that I did.

My own, right beside Borus the Kinslayer in the final match of the day.

CHAPTER 4

I spent the rest of the day tucked away in my cell listening to men die.

The roar of the crowd mingled with the screams of the defeated and dismembered to soak down through my ceiling like cold water. All I could do was huddle on my pallet and try to keep the rising panic in my gut from spreading out to the rest of me, but it was better than enduring the constant staring and whispering I'd been getting in the mess hall. It seemed word had gotten around. I didn't have much appetite for lunch, but I tried to keep my head down and eat a meal just to keep my strength up.

Even Alleron had seemed far less cheerful. He kept muttering about how "it wasn't supposed to happen this way" and "how could I have missed this?" until I finally snapped and told him to stow the chatter before I stuffed my bowl in his mouth. My anger seemed to snap him out of whatever fog he'd been in. He stared at me for a moment, then shrugged and broke out the glowing smile he normally kept firmly lodged on his face.

"You're right of course. When faced with the unexpected we must simply find a way to make the best of things until events resolve themselves onto a clear path once more."

He nodded as though he'd arrived at some important decision, then began shouting over the mess hall's noise that he was now taking wagers on my chances. Soon he had more toughs lined up to place bets than you'd find beggars outside a Vestan temple on festival day. I took the opportunity to slip off to my room. At least there I could have a proper nervous breakdown in private.

I'm not sure exactly how long I waited, but it was long enough that I actually felt relieved when a loud knock on my door announced that my turn in the arena had arrived. As I stood to unlock the door I wondered if anyone had ever tried to just sit tight and pretend no one was home. The bolt would hold them back for a while, but I knew Cael carried a master key, and the other guards would not take kindly to being forced to call him. I undid the latch and found to my surprise that it was Cael himself who waited for me on the other side.

He nodded a greeting, but didn't speak as he turned and walked to the nearby door that formed the end of the hallway. Now it stood open, and I saw that the floor beyond slanted upwards towards sunlight and echoed with the shouts, cheers, and screams I'd been hearing all day long. Once we stepped through the door, I saw that a room stood to my right and left at the base of the ramp. The room to my right reeked of blood and fear, and I caught a glimpse of men writhing on tables as a harried medicus and his assistants tried to save those they could. I turned away before my stomach got the better of me, and was relieved when Cael turned and stepped into the room on my left.

That feeling of relief faded fast once I had a chance to look around. The room was filled with more implements of death than I'd ever seen in one place before. Swords, spears, axes, shields, and a whole host of weapons whose name and purpose I couldn't begin to guess at stood in shining rows on tables and filled racks on the wall.

"Take your pick," Cael said as he gestured around the room. "You can use whatever you can carry."

As I looked around the room the last bit of hope I'd clung to drained out of me in a hurry. I knew how to handle myself well enough. You don't survive Byzantia's streets without becoming at least passingly acquainted with violence. I'd busted a few heads and broken a few noses, even knifed a guy once when he decided he'd rather kill me than share our haul, though I'd let him live to tell about it.

But for the most part I'd kept my skin in one piece by avoiding the kinds of situations that called for weapons like these. They can't kill what they can't catch. One of the few perks of life as a nameless street waif is that you're not burdened by any honor worth defending in the first place, so turning tail at the first sign of trouble is usually the best way to stay alive. With gods only knew how much earth, stone, and locked doors standing between me and freedom running wasn't exactly an option. Soon I'd be fighting for my life against a very motivated bruiser with a taste for blood and more practice with blades like these than I could hope to match even if they'd given me a year to train.

"Don't suppose you have time for a quick lesson?" I asked Cael with a weak smile. I'd meant it as a joke, but he nodded like he'd been hoping I'd ask all along and led me over to a table loaded with rows of gleaming swords and daggers.

"Forget about the heavy stuff," he said as he picked up a longsword, tested its balance, then returned it to the table. "That's what Borus will bring, but he's got more strength, skill, and instinct than you can ever hope to match."

"Thanks for the encouraging words."

"It's only the plain truth. Hiding from it won't save you, but heeding it might. He's strong, but you're fast. He's got experience, but he'll think you an easy victory, which means he'll try to make a show of killing you to please the crowd."

He selected a short legion gladius and handed it to me. I gave it a quick twirl and had to admit that the balance felt better than I'd expected.

"What about something longer, like those spears over there?"

As soon as Cael turned towards where I was pointing I slipped a dagger off the table and tucked it into my boot. I was grateful for his help, I truly was, but I hadn't forgotten that he was Trebonious' right hand man. I didn't think he was likely to go reporting on my preparations, but it was my life on the line, so I saw no sense in finding out the hard way.

"I understand the instinct, but in close is where you want to be," he said as he turned back to me. "He's a cocky sod, so he might just give you an opening. If he does, strike hard and make it count, because he won't give you a second one."

I nodded, but I doubted any of his advice would do me much good. It sounded nice in theory, but I'd seen enough of fighting to know that all the planning in the world is worth less than a bent Drangian copper when your heart is pounding in your ears and someone is after your blood. Once the fighting started I was going to give it everything I had, but that didn't mean I was feeling optimistic about my chances.

Cael must have sensed some of what I was feeling, because he put his hand on my shoulder and opened his mouth to say something else.

"Fighters, to your stations!" the baritone voice of the fight announcer rumbled down the ramp and echoed through the room.

Cael closed his mouth, thought for a moment, then nodded as if he'd made some sort of decision.

"Grass rise up to meet you. Sky reach down to hold you. Stand tall, fight well, die with honor."

His words sent a small shiver through my bones, and I could tell they held a special meaning to him. Just then the urge to cry hit me harder than any time I could remember since I'd been a girl of six hiding from Mother Shanti's temper beneath the cloister stairs. I stuffed the feeling down into my gut before it reached my eyes, smiled up at him, then turned and walked towards the door.

I'll be damned if your last memory of me is nothing but tear stains and snot.

I got a hold of myself again by the time I reached the door and paused to look back over my shoulder.

"Can I ask a favor of you?"

"You can ask. Can't promise I'll grant it."

"If Borus kills me, take a piss in his beer for me."

Cael's laughter echoed from the cold stone walls and followed me up the ramp as I marched my way towards the arena sands.

***

"You know his name, you know his deeds. Good sirs and dames, I give you Borus the Kinslayer, Farshore's Arena Champion!"

The center of the arena floor was occupied by a circle of tall stone pillars that blocked my view of its far side, but the steady din of shouts and cheers that filled the stands rose to a deafening roar as Borus entered. Alleron had said the man had earned the title Kinslayer after he killed both of his brothers over a woman back in Byzantia. Trebonious had claimed him for the arena before he'd taken two steps off the dock. Since then Borus had won so many victories that Trebonious rarely scheduled matches for him anymore, so the crowd had learned to expect a great show when they heard his name ring out.

"And now, fresh from the old world, Charity of Byzantia stands ready to fight for your entertainment!"

The announcer's voice was amplified by the announcer's booth. It swept up his words and flung them around the circular walls, but I still almost missed my cue over the roar of the crowd in the stands. The guard nudged me with his elbow, I took a deep breath, and stepped out from the shade of the tunnel onto the arena sands.

The heat of the sun and the crash of sound all around hit me like a blow to the head. I'd seen fighters back home cheer, wave, or salute their fans as they entered the arena, but it was all I could do to put one foot in front of the other without falling over. As I walked forward the crowd's cheers began to die away, until all I heard was the quiet buzz of confused questions and muttered disappointment. I couldn't make out one voice from the next, but I could guess what they were saying all the same.

"What's that slip of a girl doing on the sand with our champion?"

"Has Trebonious lost his mind?"

"We waited all day for this?"

Nothing about this match made sense, and the crowd knew it. They paid good coin to watch a contest worthy of the Divines, and even I wasn't stupid or hopeful enough to think they were about to get one.

I looked up into the glare of the sun and saw Governor Caligus sitting in the shade of his private box, cradling a cup of wine in his hand and grinning down at me like a desert jackal.

Well, at least now I know who I have to thank for all this.

I should have realized what was going on the moment I saw my name besides Borus' on the list. I'd embarrassed the governor in front of Farshore's most influential citizens. He couldn't just let that pass without losing face, and it seemed he was willing to anger the arena crowd in order to make a very painful and public example of me to his lords and ladies.

I scowled up at him and spat on the ground, then turned back to the arena floor and put the governor out of my mind. He might be the reason I was standing here, but he wasn't the one who was about to try and kill me. That honor went to the muscle-bound brute who stepped around a pillar and started walking towards me across the open sand.

Borus was clad in a pair of linen breeches, naked from the waist up and carrying a wicked-looking battle axe in each hand. I'd seen several suits of leather and metal armor in the armory. I'd ignored them because they were either too big or too heavy to be worth the trouble, but Borus could easily have worn any of them. The fact that he chose to face me with his scarred and tattooed chest exposed was the clearest sign I'd seen yet of just how bad my chances truly were.

As he drew closer I could tell from the look on his face that Borus was no more pleased to be here than I was, though for very different reasons. The crowd's muttering had grown louder, and I even heard a few boos ripple through the stands. Borus scowled, twirled his axes a few times, and settled into a fighting stance, clearly eager to get this over with and put it behind him.

"Warriors!" the announcer's voice boomed across the sands. "In the name of the Five Divines, fight with honor, die with courage, live on in glory. Begin!"

Borus came for me before the words had faded from the air, swinging his axes in a crescent swipe meant to take my head clean off my shoulders.

Thankfully, I ducked.

He turned his strike into a flurry of wild blows, swinging and chopping in a frenzy of muscles and rage. I spun, twisted, and dodged on pure instinct. I knew better than to try to block his wild swings with my sword. The force he put behind each one would have crushed through my guard in an instant, but it also meant that the momentum of each swipe carried his arms out to the side for a moment before he could recover. I watched and waited, getting a feel for his rhythm as I kept one step ahead of death. Then he swung just a little too wide.

I ducked beneath his blade and struck out at his exposed rib cage. The wind from his axe tugged at my hair as I felt the shock of my sword striking flesh.

If my blade had been a few inches longer it would have been the end of the fight altogether. Instead it only left a long red gash across his right side. Painful, no doubt, but not fatal. Which meant I was almost certainly a dead woman standing.

"First blood! First blood to the Byzantian Battle Queen!"

I thought that was stretching things a bit far, but the crowd went wild, screaming and hollering at the sight of the arena champion humbled by a girl half his size. Borus touched two fingers to the wound and raised them in front of his face, now dripping red. He stared at them for a moment, as if his mind couldn't accept what had just happened. When he looked back at me his eyes were pure murder.

This time when he charged he kept his anger locked up tight, and I got a close up view of the cold, ruthless skill that had ended countless lives on this very spot. His blows were short, controlled, and powerful now, leaving nothing exposed and giving little warning before they struck home. It was all I could do to stay a hair's breadth away from the razor edges of his axes, and any thought of counter attacking quickly faded from my mind.

My breath started to burn in my lungs, and I realized that it was only a matter of time before one of his swings caught up with me. The only thing I had left to try was something so stupid he would never expect it. Fortunately, reckless and stupid is a Charity specialty.

When the next swipe came at my head, I threw myself into a backwards somersault to gain some distance. I took quick aim as I rolled to my feet, then threw my sword at his chest with all the strength I could muster. The blade spun end over end in a deadly spiral that sent his eyes wide with shock as it flashed towards him. It was a good throw. If I'd faced off against an average fighter then I'm sure the shock of my unexpected attack would have bought my sword the split second it needed to bury itself in his heart. But Borus was anything but an average fighter.

He twisted aside with impossible speed, and the tip of my sword only grazed a shallow cut across his shoulder as it flew by. As Borus stood straight again his face lit up with a wolfish grin.

Uh oh.

Without waiting for his next move I turned and ran as fast as my legs would carry me.

Before long I heard the scuffle of feet and heavy breathing behind me. A quick glance over my shoulder confirmed that he was now hot on my heels, his axes held out away from his body on both sides like the wings of some freakish bird of prey.

I spun left as I passed a stone pillar, putting its solid bulk between me and Borus as I started running around the outer edge of the circle. The crowd began to boo as I robbed them of their glorious contest, but I didn't give two shits what they thought. As far as I was concerned, the first one of them who wanted to come down here and fight Borus himself was welcome to all the glory he could eat in one sitting. I was more concerned with staying alive than staying popular.

Still, I knew that running away had only bought me a few more minutes. On the streets you could run until you found somewhere to hide, but here in the arena there was only sand, sun, and stone pillars. I felt a whoosh of air at the back of my neck, then another, and realized that Borus had gained enough ground to try and swipe at me again.

"Aaagh! Stand and fight me like a man!" Borus roared behind me.

"Do you realize…how stupid…that sounds?" I panted back at him as I dodged around a pillar to regain some ground.

I was as good as dead if I didn't find some way to change the game in the next few minutes. My lungs were screaming at me now, my legs felt like mud, and the knife that I'd hidden in my boot dug into my ankle every time I took a step.

The knife!

Borus thought I was unarmed and defenseless now, so he wasn't bothering to guard himself anymore. A plan began to take shape, and I launched into it before I had time to think of all the many and gruesome ways it would probably get me killed.

I ran flat out for a pillar on the opposite side of the circle, willing my legs to move just a little bit faster. I risked another quick glance over my shoulder and saw that Borus was about two arm lengths behind me now, sweating and red faced but barreling towards me all the same.

Come on, you stupid ox. Come and get me.

When I was two steps away from the pillar I leapt up and used my momentum to run up its surface like I was scaling the wall of a nobleman's estate. I shot up its side until I was a good six feet in the air. Just as I felt my momentum begin to bleed away I pushed off the stone into a backflip that carried me out into open air.

Time slowed as I soared. Borus stared up at me with his mouth hanging open in disbelief as I spun over his head.

I tucked into a ball, pulled the knife from my boot, and landed on the sand in a crouch behind him. Before he could recover I lashed out with two quick strikes.

The temple library of the Daughters of Vesta contains all the knowledge worth possessing, or so Mother Shanti was fond of saying. I'd taken a special interest in the lessons on anatomy. At first that was only because the illustrations were far more interesting than another dry lecture on the history of kings and states or complex mathematical formulae. Soon I realized that understanding the way the body moves and functions offered some pretty interesting advantages. For example, Borus' legs might have been thicker than the mast of the *Typhon*, but they were connected to his feet by the ever-vulnerable Acheron's tendon, just like everyone else's. When my knife sliced through those tendons, he collapsed to his knees in a crash of dust.

I jumped to my feet, reached around in front of him, and cut his throat before he could recover.

Blood sprayed out onto the sand in a crimson fan. As the fallen arena champion toppled forward every sound in the arena died away into silence. Ten thousand faces stared down at me in shock. I felt my limbs start to tremble as the adrenaline died away and the reality of what I'd just done settled over me, but I knew that these next few moments mattered almost as much as the fight itself. I needed the crowd on my side if I hoped to survive in here much longer, and nobody enjoyed watching a girl bawl her eyes out.

I stood to my feet, pointed the bloody knife straight at Caligus, then opened my hand to let it fall to the ground. As the knife hit the floor the stands erupted in a deafening chorus of shouts, cheers, and chants that made everything that had come before it sound like polite applause. The announcer had recovered his wits enough to finally say something about the unexpected conclusion, but I couldn't hear his words over the roar that thundered all around me.

That jackal smile was gone from Caligus' face now, replaced by a beautifully sour frown that did wonders to cheer my spirits. I raised both arms over my head to salute the crowd, then spun on my heel and marched back to the tunnel I'd emerged from what now felt like a lifetime ago.

I was rather pleased that I made it all the way back to the shelter of its cool shadows before I vomited up what little remained of my breakfast.

CHAPTER 5

Dinner passed without incident. The other fighters steered clear of me after I walked out of the arena with Borus' blood on my clothes, and that suited me just fine. I stuffed food in my mouth without noticing the taste, then walked straight back to my room. Cael was waiting with a few sets of fresh clothing, along with a small table and chair to round out the decor of my cell.

He called them "the victor's reward." As far as I was concerned I was still breathing, and that was reward enough.

I slept like shit that night.

I was exhausted, but as I lay on my pallet in the darkness my thoughts kept returning to the final moments of my fight in the arena. The look of surprise on Borus' face as his brain had caught up to what was happening faster than his body could react. The grunt of pain as my knife cut into him. The spray of blood across the sand.

I told myself that I had no reason to feel guilt over taking his life. I hadn't asked for that fight, and he'd made it damned clear that he intended to kill me and enjoy himself in the process. No doubt if he'd been the one standing over my corpse he would have crowed about it to the skies, drank an extra beer that night, and forgotten my face by the morning. But all the logic in the world didn't calm my stomach or make sleep any easier.

I lost track of how many hours I'd lain there when I finally gave up, pulled my new linen shirt over my head, and stepped out into the hall.

Everything was quiet. By my guess it was still the small hours of the morning so I doubted that the kitchens would be serving breakfast yet. Still, since I had nowhere else to go I decided to go claim myself a bench so that I could be sure I'd get one of the first plates they sent out. Seemed better than laying awake in the dark trying to keep my hands from shaking.

Given the early hour I assumed the main hall would be empty. I was wrong. The big orc I'd seen around a few times before sat alone at a table by the wall. She had her back turned towards me, but turned to look over her shoulder as I walked into the room even though I was sure I hadn't made a sound. She frowned, but scooted over on the bench and nodded to the seat beside her.

"I like to come here early to enjoy the silence before things get too crowded, but you may join me if you feel inclined towards company."

Her voice was deep and soothing. She spoke Byzantian with a strange, clipped accent, but she spoke it better than many alleycats I'd heard jabbering on back home. I couldn't help but glance nervously at her pointed teeth as she spoke. The two longer tusks that rose up from her jaw looked like they could punch through steel if she tried hard enough, but even I knew that moving to sit somewhere else would have been incredibly rude after such a civil welcome. I swallowed hard, nodded, and moved to join her.

"Your name is Nataka, right?"

She nodded.

"I'm Charity."

"So I have heard."

I wasn't sure if I should be flattered or concerned by that as I slid onto the bench. No sooner had I sat down than she stood to her feet.

"The cook was kind enough to brew some tea while he waited for the ovens to heat up. I will bring you some."

She disappeared through the kitchen door, then returned a few minutes later carrying two steaming cups. She set one down in front of me as she returned to her seat, then took a careful sip from her own mug and let out a contented sigh.

"Fresh-brewed Skariam leaf. If there is a better way to begin the morning, then I have not found it."

I blew on my tea for a bit, then took a sip. It was surprisingly spicy, with a hint of citrus and honey, and damn if it didn't leave me feeling a little bit better. We sat in silence for a while, enjoying our drinks and not bothering each other. I sat on a bench beside a monster out of the legends, and it was by far the calmest and most pleasant ten minutes I'd experienced in a long, long time.

"My people tell stories of your kind."

I jumped a little as her rumbling voice broke the stillness, then looked up at her.

"Oh? I didn't think there were any humans here in Danan before Tiberius and his fleet arrived."

"There weren't. But I think that there must have been, once. Legends speak of a strange race who once lived along the shore. Slower than elves, weaker than dwarves, more timid than halflings, yet far more dangerous than any of them in large numbers."

I blinked. That was news to me.

"That might have been humans, I suppose. What happened to them?"

"The legends only say that they vanished long ago. Until your kind returned to our shores I'd thought them nothing more than strange stories for children."

"Ha. Yeah, that's pretty much what we think of you."

"Is it true that none but your own kind live in your homeland?"

She furrowed her brow as I nodded, appearing more thoughtful than angry.

"It must be a strange thing to know nothing but peace."

"What?"

She tilted her head to one side and gave me a strange look.

"Did I use your words incorrectly? If you live only among your own kind, then you have no war, correct?"

Somehow I managed to catch myself before I laughed out loud.

"Um, no. We humans can find an excuse for war faster than a dog can sniff out shit. If the kingdoms aren't fighting, then they're scheming about how to start a fight to their best advantage. Orcs don't fight amongst themselves?"

She shook her head.

"One orc may fight with another. Blood debts must always be settled and young blood will always seek to test itself, but that is not the same as war."

"A noble conflict is the greatest teacher, for it reveals the nature of man to himself."

"Wise words for one so young."

"Thanks," I grinned, "but they aren't mine. That was Epicus, a third era philosopher. He was big on instilling virtue, so Mother Shanti made me read his work twice."

From the way she stared at me you'd have thought I'd just said I like to eat babies for breakfast.

"You are *Gelerhtag*?"

"I'm sorry?"

"Ack, your words are too small for such a large thing. *Gelerhtag* is a vessel of knowledge, a keeper of the old wisdom and a teller of tales. They are the greatest and most respected among my kin."

"That's definitely not me then."

"But you can read your people's script?"

I nodded.

"And write it as well?"

"Yeah, although Mother Shanti always said my scribbles were so ugly that it was unfair to scribes to call them writing."

She grinned. Our conversation hadn't made her teeth any less unsettling.

"That is the second time you've mentioned her. She sounds like a wise woman."

"Sure," I said, not bothering to hide the bitterness in my voice. "She was a peach."

"She is dead, your mother?"

"She's not—" I paused, unsure of how to explain my strange relationship with the woman who had raised me, then abandoned me. Then I decided it wasn't worth trying. The old hag had been cold, distant, uncompromising, and ruthless. She had also been by far the closest thing I'd ever had to a real mother, and that sad truth was more than I could handle on an empty stomach.

"I honestly don't know if she's dead or not, but she might as well be as far as I'm concerned."

Nataka frowned, but seemed to know when to leave well enough alone. We sat in silence once again until the hall began to fill behind us. Finally, she finished the last of her tea and stood to her feet.

"I hope we are never matched against one another on the list, young Charity. It would sadden me to kill a *Gelerhtag* of your people. Even one with poor penmanship."

She dipped her head in a solemn bow, then turned and walked out the door before I could think of a proper response.

The common room continued to fill as the other fighters gathered for breakfast. A guard brought me a bowl of porridge and an apple. No one bothered to join me, which suited me just fine. I ate without giving the food much thought, focusing instead on the strange conversation I'd just had with an orc. She wasn't anything like what I'd expected, which I was coming to suspect was going to be true of many things here in Farshore.

Her reaction to learning that I was literate had taken me especially by surprise. I suppose that reading and writing were rare enough skills to find in Byzantia's gutters. Most were too busy hunting down their next meal to make the time to learn, even if there'd been someone willing to teach. No doubt I'd have been the same if the Daughters of Vesta hadn't made consistent improvement in the academic sciences a condition of remaining within their walls and eating their food.

But Nataka had seemed more than just impressed. From the way she'd spoken of it you'd have thought that reading and writing was a sacred thing. I wonder how she'd have felt if she knew what else was rattling around in my brain?

Stories, poems, formulae, detailed medical recipes and more had been jostling and squabbling over headspace since the day I first walked through the temple gates. I often worried that I was becoming a modern day Archicus, the thief who managed to unlock the gates of Charydis to steal from the gods. He stole so much from Vesta's table that he forgot how to feed himself and starved to death once he returned home. Sister Jesra had been especially fond of that tale, and the moral that went along with it; a little knowledge can be a dangerous thing.

I sighed, pushed away my empty bowl and stood to my feet. I hadn't thought about the temple in years, but my thoughts seemed inclined to return there often since I'd arrived in Farshore. It seemed that losing the sad excuse for a life that I'd built for myself was dragging up memories of the last time I'd been forced to start again with nothing but what I could carry in my head. Still, I had to admit that even the Daughters' endless rules and lectures were more pleasant to dwell on than the recent monopoly that blood and death had maintained on my thoughts, so that was something.

"Well, well. Here she is in the flesh."

I turned to find myself face to face with a pack of scowling thugs. I looked them over, instantly alert.

Four men. Their Byzantian short-cropped hair said "ex-legion," the fact that it had only just begun to grow out again said that they'd been tossed out recently, and the ugly in their eyes said they'd earned their discharge the hard way.

"You boys come here often?"

They grinned at my weak joke, but there was no laughter in their eyes. The one in the lead leaned in a little, close enough to give me a whiff of his sour breath as he growled an answer.

"Aye, that we do. Used to share a meal here every morning with the finest man I've ever known. His name was Borus, and a two-copper whore like you weren't fit to clean up his shit, let alone enter the ring with him."

I tossed a quick glance at the nearest guard. He was talking with two men seated at a table against the far wall. Even if I screamed it would be ten seconds or more before he caught up to what was happening and made it across the room to intervene, and I was well aware of just how much damage a few motivated bruisers could do in ten seconds.

"Funny you should mention whores," I said to keep their eyes on me as I reached around behind my back.

"Borus asked a favor of me before we faced off. Maybe you could help me honor his wishes?"

"Oh?" They looked at each other, unsure of how to respond. My fingers found the spoon I'd left in my empty bowl. I closed a fist over the round end to leave the metal handle sticking out through my knuckles. If I could take one down fast it might slow the others long enough for the guard to get involved. Or make them mad enough to crack my skull open instead of just breaking my face a bit, but any chance seemed better than just standing still and waiting for the pain to start. I cleared my throat and spit on the lead basher's foot.

"Yep. Turns out he fucked your mother last night, but hadn't gotten around to paying her yet. You don't happen to have a coin to spare, do you?"

His eyes went wide, then lit with rage as he pulled back his fist.

Perfect.

I jumped toward the opening he'd given me and punched my makeshift dagger at his throat. Even the blunt end of a spoon handle can do some serious damage if you land it hard enough in the right spot. I have no doubt that it would have done just that if his head hadn't jerked out of the way just as I began my swing. He flew past me as I swiped at empty air. I caught the look of surprise on his face before it was slammed down onto the table behind me.

His friends and I stared at their fallen comrade. Our eyes looked from his bleeding face to his arm twisted tight in its socket, and finally to the dwarf who held his wrist in an iron grip and glared back up at us with fire in his eyes.

"Hey! Break that up!"

The dwarf looked over his shoulder at the approaching guard without letting go.

"We're just talking."

He didn't shout, but the warning in his voice was clear. The guard opened his mouth to snap a reply, then caught himself and glanced around the room. Two more were on their way. He pointed his club at the dwarf, but didn't move any closer.

"Let him go, Magnus."

"I just told the good soldier here that we're only having a friendly chat," Magnus growled as he twisted the thug's arm a little tighter. "Now, are we just talking? Or do you plan to make a liar out of me?"

"Aye!" the man yelped as he rose up onto his toes. "Just talking!"

"That's a lad," Magnus said as he let go of the man's arm and patted his head like a puppy who'd just taken a shit outside for the first time. The bruiser stood to his feet, rolled his shoulder with a wince of pain, then shot a final glare at me before storming off towards the training hall with his friends trailing after him. The guard nodded and turned to walk back to his post by the door, but not before I caught the look of relief that flashed across his face.

"Thanks," I said as I turned to my unexpected rescuer, "but I could have handled—"

"Don't," he snapped as he held up a hand.

"Don't what?"

"Don't thank me. I wasn't helping you, so don't waste your words."

"Mind telling me what you were doing, then?"

"Just staking my claim."

"Pardon?" I didn't like the sound of that.

He sighed and shook his head.

"That Borus was a right bastard, but he was also the only halfway decent challenge in this rotten hole. The thought of facing him in honest combat was one of the last decent ways I had of passing the hours, until you got to him first. So now I'm forced to settle for killing you, instead. Your blood doesn't deserve to grace my axe, but if I'm going to be forced to make do then I'll be damned if I let some dog turd with a grudge leave you any weaker than you already are before we face off in the arena."

He looked me over from top to toe, then shook his head again and turned to march off to a different table.

"Nice to meet you too," I called after him. He took a seat, grabbed a bowl, and set about ignoring my existence.

I looked around the room. Everyone else was following his lead. Back when I ran Byzantia's streets I would have kissed a Novari yak for the power to turn invisible, but just then it was beginning to grow rather old. I scowled, turned my back on the room, and went in search of something to fill up the rest of what was starting to look like a very long day.

CHAPTER 6

"Blood is spilled! Honor is given! Lords and dames, cheer for the victor!"

The announcer's voice boomed down the ramp as I stepped into the armory once again to find Cael already waiting for me. My restlessness had grown so bad over the past week that I actually felt a flood of relief when he'd appeared in the training room that morning to post the list for the new games and I'd found my name on it. I wasn't eager to risk my life again, but at least it meant that something was happening. The strange bit was that there was no opponent listed next to my name, just the word "challenge" in bold letters. I had no idea what that meant, but I hoped that I might not have to spill blood in order to survive for another day.

Now that I heard the dying screams of whoever had just lost that fight mixed with the roar of the crowd overhead I was feeling decidedly less excited.

"Now enjoy yourselves while the next combatant makes their final preparations. Eat, drink, and place your wagers, for the contest you are about to witness will be unlike anything you have ever seen before."

I didn't love the sound of that, but my turn on the sands had come whether I was ready or not. I smiled at Cael and offered him a nod in greeting. He didn't smile back. In fact, he looked like someone had snuck sawdust into his breakfast when he wasn't looking.

"Choose your weapon," he said as he pointed to the many options around the room.

"Any suggestions? The list didn't name my opponent, so I don't know what I'm dealing with."

"I am not permitted to advise the combatants on their preparations." His face was as blank and cold as the stone walls.

Ah. Sounds like someone got a bit of a talking to after my last fight.

I guess it made sense that Trebonious had looked for a scapegoat to vent his frustrations on after a nameless girl had taken down his star fighter. He had no way of knowing that I'd kept the knife hidden from Cael, too. It wasn't fair that he'd gotten in trouble for it. Then again, it wasn't fair that I was being forced to fight for my life while he got to stay safe down here and sulk, so I wasn't feeling an abundance of sympathy just then.

"Right. My mistake."

I sighed and picked up the same gladius I'd carried when I fought Borus. Without any information to go on I didn't see any reason to choose something else. I gave the blade a quick once over, then turned for the door.

"Wait."

I turned to find Cael staring at the ground. He chewed at his lip for a moment, opened his mouth to say something, then seemed to think better of it. He looked up at me, and I saw genuine concern in his eyes.

"If you're going to wish me luck now would be a good time. Got an appointment to keep, and from the look on your face I think I'm going to need it."

That earned me a small smile. Then he nodded once and turned to look at a rack of polearms on the wall next to him. He reached up and took down a short spear. The shaft was only about four feet long, but the blade on the end added another foot of sharpened steel that looked more like the straight blade of a dagger than the leaf-shaped tips I'd seen on legion spears.

"This is called a *haska*. It's a Gallean weapon, though not one most warriors would choose to wield. Our women train with them. It gives good reach, and the blade lets you cut as well as thrust."

I smiled, then nodded like I used to when I sat through one of Sister Gizella's lectures.

"Very interesting. You know, I am struck by the sudden and completely unpredictable desire to try out this fascinating weapon for myself. In the interest of cultural exploration, you understand."

He smiled back and tossed the spear to me. I caught it out of the air and gave it a quick twirl. I could see what he meant. The center of balance made quick swipes and stabs much easier, even with my lighter frame.

"Of course, they always wield it with a shield," he said as he lifted one from a table and carried it over to me.

"If it's good enough for a Gallean housewife then it's good enough for me."

"Your arm goes here."

He took my hand and guided it through the leather straps. His fingers were callused from a lifetime of sword drills, but surprisingly gentle as he helped me fit the shield in place. It was made of sturdy oak with an iron rim, an iron boss at the center, and was wrapped in cured leather. I was surprised to find that it was lighter than I'd expected once I had it secured onto my arm.

"Stay low, move fast, and keep your shield up," he said as he squeezed my shoulder.

"Always. And thank you."

He nodded as I headed for the door and marched up the ramp to see what Trebonious had in store for me this time.

I shielded my eyes from the sun's glare as I reached the top of the ramp and looked out into the arena. There was nothing there. The pillars that had stood there previously were gone, and all I saw now was empty sand.

"Now entering the arena for the second time, the slayer of champions and battle queen of Byzantia, Charity!"

I took my cue and stepped out into the sunlight. This time the crowd cheered my entrance. I had no doubt that the story of my fight with Borus had made its way round the city by now. I looked around, but still saw no sign of my opponent. But now that my eyes had adjusted I saw that the arena wasn't as empty as I'd first thought. A large wooden tub sat to my right, filled to the brim with water, while a decent sized stack of firewood stood on my left.

"My lords and dames, you are about to enjoy a contest unique in the history of the arena, a battle not of flesh against flesh, but one of strength and skill pitted against the fury of the elements themselves."

I still didn't have any clue what he was talking about, but I knew there was no way it could be good for my continued health. Before I had a chance to do much of anything a figure emerged from the shade of the governor's box. As I squinted up at it I realized that it was an elf, and a female at that. She wore flowing robes of black and red that matched her onyx hair, and I noticed an intricate pattern of tattooed patterns spiraling up her neck to snake around her eyes.

She stared down at me for a moment, then smirked, knelt on the floor of the stand, and closed her eyes. The arena door slammed shut behind me as I walked out to the center of the arena.

"Warrior!" The announcer's voice shattered the eager hush that had fallen over the crowd. "In the name of the Five Divines, fight with honor, die with courage, live on in glory. Begin!"

As his voice echoed across the sand an archer stepped up next to the woman. The tip of his arrow danced with a smoldering flame as he pulled back his bowstring, took aim, and fired. I raised my shield, but the flaming missile shot to my left to bury itself in the woodpile. The wood must have been treated with oil, because it roared into a full bonfire in an instant. The archer stepped back into the shadows, and I turned in a slow circle as I searched for whatever was coming to kill me.

Nothing moved. A breeze teased at my hair as the fire snapped and popped beside me. The crowd began to mutter and whisper as they waited for something to happen, but the elf still knelt with her eyes closed, and the door to the other arena entranced remained shut.

Then I felt it.

The hairs on my neck prickled to life as the breeze died away. A whisper tickled my ear, but when I spun around I found nothing there. My senses screamed that there was someone standing beside me even though my eyes were certain that I was alone. If there had been shadows I would have searched them for signs of someone hiding there, but the bright sun had long since burned them all away.

Then the fire exploded behind me. A wave of hot air sent me stumbling forward. I spun around to find pieces of smoldering firewood scattered across the sand, with only a bed of glowing coals where the bonfire had stood. Then a hand burst up out of the embers.

It was the same size and shape as a human hand but was formed of black rock shot through with veins of fire that pulsed an angry crimson. It slammed to the ground, dug its fingers into the sand, and pulled. A head pushed up through the coals, then a pair of shoulders and another hand like the first. The head had no face, only two eyes that glowed like embers at the heart of a forge as the creature gave one final heave and hauled itself up out of the earth. It pushed up onto its knees, then stood to its feet.

I heard a loud splash behind me and whirled around to find another man-sized figure standing where the tub of water had been. Broken planks and bits of bent hooping littered the sand around the shimmering, translucent body.

A woman screamed in the stands, and her voice broke the spell of silence that had gripped the crowd. People stood and began pushing their way towards the exits as they sought to escape the sudden and unexpected display of magic.

"Fear not, good citizens of Farshore!" the announcer shouted over the rising panic. "Rest assured that the magic you see before you is kept well in hand, and has been sanctioned by Jovian's prelate for your entertainment. Behold! A contest unlike any this arena has ever seen unfolds before you."

I saw some continue their flight, but for most their curiosity overcame their caution. The stands refilled and the good men and women of Farshore redoubled their frenzied cheers and screams. I cast a quick glance up at the elf woman. I had no idea how any of this was even possible, but I was sure she was responsible for it somehow. She opened her eyes and looked down at me as if she had felt my gaze on her. They were completely black. The sight of two bottomless pools of ink staring down at me where her eyes should have been unnerved me far more than her creatures had managed.

Then she screamed. It was a long, shrieking cry of fury and rage, and suddenly the two creatures echoed the cry and rushed at me.

"See how elemental beings respond to the enchantress' very will!"

I jumped backward to avoid being caught between them, but the elementals charged in on me with abandon. Fire swung a fist at my head while

Water swept a low kick at my legs. I got my shield up and deflected the punch in a shower of sparks just as the column of water knocked my legs out from under me. I scrambled back as I hit the sand, rolling out of the way just as two fists struck the spot where I'd lain. Sand exploded in a shower of steam and the two elementals stumbled back from the blast, giving me enough time to scramble to my feet.

I was ready for their next attack. I put all the impossible magic shit out of my mind and focused on fighting as if they were just two humans with a skin condition. I dodged to the left as they charged at me, slashed my spear through Water's torso, then spun it around and drove the blade into Fire's chest.

The crowd gasped as Water clutched his chest and stumbled backward. The gash I'd opened with my spear flowed together like water poured into a bowl. The spear was ripped from my fingers, and I turned to see Fire toss it away from him. He'd pulled the blade from his chest like I'd just stuck him with a sewing needle. I'd just struck them each with what should have been a fatal hit, but I didn't see any sign that they'd even felt it.

This wasn't a battle. It was an execution.

For the second time in my arena career I turned around and ran like hell. This time the crowd screamed encouragements instead of booing me. Seemed that they'd taken my side against the inhuman monsters that were now chasing after me, but their support didn't do me a damned bit of good.

A flaming rock singed my ear as it shot by an inch from my head to explode against the arena wall. I looked back to see Fire conjure another missile and launch it straight at me. I spun around and got my shield up just before it hit me. Fire swept around me, burning my shins as the force of the blast sent me stumbling backward.

Then Water burst through the cloud of smoke. His arms now ended in shimmering blades of ice where his hands had been, and he slashed them both at my head as he ran forward. I deflected one strike with my shield as I ducked beneath the second.

Suddenly a column of water flowed around my shield and struck me in the face. It surged into my nose and mouth and forced its way into my lungs. The shield was ripped from my arm as I flew up into the air. I looked down to see that Water held me in the air, his hand covering my face as my feet dangled above the sand. I couldn't breathe, and my efforts to do so only sucked more water down my throat. I clawed and scratched at his arm as my vision began to blur and blacken, but my fingers passed harmlessly through him.

I was three heartbeats away from Magren's door, and there wasn't a damned thing I could do about it.

Another explosion of steam threw me backwards to slam into the wall and fall to the ground. I'm sure it would have knocked all the air out of me if I'd had any left. I coughed up a bucketful of water and sucked down a huge gasping breath. Then I heard a long shriek of pain ring out through the arena and looked up to see Water standing there with his arm and most of his shoulder missing, then past him to where Fire stood with another flaming missile ready in his hands. He must have thrown one at me just as Water picked me up, and struck his friend instead of me.

The scream had belonged to a woman, though. I looked over their heads to where the elven woman knelt in the governor's box. She clutched her head in her hands as if she fought off the worst headache in the history of hangovers. It seemed her little toys didn't play so well together, and she seemed to feel it when that happened. She shook her head and glared down at me, her black eyes full of fury as she pointed a finger at my heart and screamed another wordless scream of rage.

Fire and Water leapt back into action, racing towards me at her command. I still had no way to fight them, but I thought I saw a slim chance to strike at the witch directly. It would probably still get me killed, but at least I'd give her a bloody nose on the way down.

I scrambled to my feet, but this time I ran towards the duo instead of away from them. The crowd cheered as I charged forward, then dove beneath Water's kick to scoop up my shield. I raised it just in time to block Fire's fist as it swept down at my head. The blow drove me down to one knee, and I rolled forward just as his second fist smashed the ground. I leapt up, squared my feet, and slammed my shield into Fire's back.

The heat that radiated off of him was incredible. The rim of my shield began to glow, and I knew that the treated leather was all that kept it from catching fire, although that wouldn't last much longer. I dug my toes into the sand, screamed out all the fear and anger that coursed through me, and threw myself forward.

Fire and I stumbled forward together and collided with Water as he ran towards me.

My world dissolved in a flash of white. I flew through the air for what felt like a lifetime, then hit the ground hard. I lay there gasping on the sand like a fresh-caught fish while I waited for the world to stop spinning. If my little gambit had failed then I knew the elementals would be coming to finish the job, but I was too tired to care or do much about it. The skin on my arms and legs throbbed with fire. Breathing hurt. Everything hurt, actually, but I finally forced myself up onto my elbows to take a look around.

Two black scorch marks in the sand were all that remained of Fire and Water. I looked up at the governor's stand. The elf lay slumped on the ground. Steam rose from her ears and open mouth. Her eyes had cleared, but now they just stared sightlessly ahead in shock.

The arena was so quiet that I could hear birds singing in the trees beyond the wall. No one moved. Now that the shock had worn off, the reality of what had just happened began to crash down on me. I'd just seen someone wield the kind of magic that was only supposed to exist in a children's tale, and she'd very nearly killed me with it. My hands began to tremble, but I stuffed it down and forced myself up to my feet. All I wanted in the world just then was to make it back to my cell and lock the door so I could have a proper breakdown in peace.

"Unbelievable! The Byzantian Battle Queen has beaten the odds once more. Truly she is favored by the Divines themselves!"

The crowd erupted in a storm of shouting, waving, stamping, and screaming as the announcer finally recovered his wits. Men and women hugged one another, and I saw more than a few tear-stained faces as thousands of people made the sign of

Jovian's Wise Eye in salute. Seemed the sight of a helpless human girl winning out over evil magic had really brightened their day.

I scowled and started walking towards the exit. The Divines didn't have two shits to do with it. I'd gotten lucky, and I knew exactly how close I'd come to never seeing another sunrise. The crowd chanted my name, but I didn't care. I had exactly one thought in my head as I stepped through the arena doors and began to limp down the ramp back to the arena pits.

Time to get the hells out of this madhouse.

Chapter 7

At first I hadn't really felt the cuts and burns I'd taken in that final blast, but damn if they weren't screaming at me by the time I'd reached the bottom of the ramp. The medicus who tended me said I'd been lucky. If the force of the explosion hadn't thrown me backwards before the steam had time to really do its work I would have been in far worse shape, but it was hard to feel grateful as he slathered stinging salve on my skin and wrapped a set of bandages around the burns. I tried to fight the blackness that pressed in on me. An alleycat's worst nightmare is to be laid out sleeping and helpless while a pack of men you don't know loom over you, but soon the pain grew so bad that it sent me spiraling down into unconsciousness.

I'm not sure how long I was out, but when I jolted awake from the nightmare I'd been having I found myself laying on the cot in my cell. I was tired, sore, angry, and really damned sick of the arena. All I could think of as I walked off the arena sands was getting the hells out of there while my limbs were still attached to my body. It seemed like my brain hadn't stopped thinking about it even as I lay there snoring, because by the time I woke up it had a plan ready and waiting for me. I was going to escape or die trying, and now I was pretty sure I knew how and when to do it.

I gave myself a week to heal while I gathered what I needed. I made a mental note that if I ever had to go and get myself injured again, the arena pits was probably the best place to do it. I'd been hurt bad before, and finding a quiet hole to lick your wounds and heal was never easy when you still had to find food and keep a wary eye out for anyone looking to take you for a free ride at the same time. Trebonious had tried his best to kill me twice, but I had to admit that he did a damned fine job of patching me up afterward. He sent a medicus to check my burns for signs of rot and change out the bandage and salve each day. By the end of the week a few patches of itchy red skin were all I had left to show for my recent brush with death.

At first I just ate a lot and slept even more. Walking hurt like the fifth hell at first, but every day the pain faded a bit more, and by the end of the week I could even stand a short round of exercise in the training room without crying. I spent my time making sure my legs were back to being as strong and steady as I could get them, and that I could keep up a decent running pace for five minutes or more.

My body wasn't the only thing I prepared. I slipped a fork and spoon into my boot during the dinner bustle, and spent two evenings fashioning them into a tension wrench and a set of picks. I tore one of the two blankets that a guard had delivered to my room after my last win into strips, then braided the strips into a length of rope which I kept hidden beneath my cot. It made a for a few cold nights, but that was a small price to pay. Over the final two days I hid an apple and a few pieces of bread up my sleeve to tuck away in my room. I knew I would need to hit the streets running, and that would be a lot easier if I didn't have to go searching for a meal on my first night beyond the arena walls.

I'd assumed that Trebonious would follow the same pattern as before and take a week off between games, but the clamor I heard coming from the training room one morning told me I'd been wrong. I thought I'd have more time to make my break, but I decided as I pushed through the crowd that if I saw my name on the list I'd take my chances and try to leg it before the work crews arrived to start setting up for the games. I'd planned on slipping out during the small hours and didn't much like my chances of managing it during the daytime, but I liked my odds of escaping death one more time even less.

    My guts were tied up in so many knots as Cael posted the list that it would have taken a gray-haired sailor to untie them, but to my surprise my name wasn't on it. I stumbled back to my room in a haze of relief, and determined to make my move that night so as not to tempt fate any farther. Even if I had been inclined to wait, the shouts and screams that echoed through my room all evening would have pushed me over the edge for sure.

    Once I heard the last door slam shut down the hallway I counted to one hundred, then gathered up my supplies and slipped outside. I'd already confirmed that they didn't post a guard in the hall after the fighters had turned in for the night. A guard stayed by the exit that connected the common room to the hallway leading up past Trebonious' office to the streets above, but why bother putting a man on the door to the arena itself when it was already locked and only led up to an empty space surrounded by twenty foot walls?

I gave the door a quick once-over, and was surprised to find that the lock barely deserved the name. I'd expected something far worse, but what I found was only a simple keyhole that turned a latch on the far side.

Am I seriously the only person who has ever tried this before?

I had the door unlocked before I'd finished that thought. I slipped through, pulled it close, and locked it again from the other side before turning to look around. The hallway was shrouded in darkness, without even the faintest bit of moonlight shining down from the top of the ramp. The doors to the armory and infirmary were both locked. I had no doubt they would have been just as easy to get into, but I already had everything I needed, and every second I lingered increased the odds that someone might happen by at exactly the wrong moment.

I headed up the ramp at a thief's pace; not a run, but more than a walk, with each step taken heel to toe to keep from making any noise. I reached the top and checked the door. This one wasn't even locked. I shook my head at the sudden run of luck and pushed it open just wide enough to slip through, then flattened myself against the wall and scanned the arena floor.

I couldn't have asked for better conditions if Vesta herself had appeared before me and offered me her aid. A light rain fell from thick clouds that hid the moon and sky overhead. The city lights beyond the wall lit the scene just well enough for me to see where I was going, but the long shadows were thick enough to swim through. Still, I held tight for another dozen heartbeats as I swept my gaze back and forth along the top of the arena wall.

Only an idiot trusted in good luck over their own senses.

Nothing moved, but I figured if anyone was unfortunate enough to be posted to guard duty on a night like this then they were likely huddled up underneath something to avoid the rain. Didn't seem like they would have thought to post a watch on the walls when they hadn't bothered to guard the door that led there. Still, being cautious hurt nothing, while being hasty might end up hurting a whole hell of a lot. I let the drizzle trickle down my face as I watched and waited.

Finally, I decided that the way really was as open as it seemed and began to slide through the shadows along the base of the wall. I followed its curve until I'd reached the far side of the arena to stand beneath the governor's box. Its wooden railing reached several feet out from the wall above the arena floor. Plenty of railing up there for something to catch on.

I untied my makeshift rope from around my waist and knotted the spoon I'd pinched to one end as a counter-weight. I spun the rope in a circle at my side, faster and faster until the momentum felt right, then launched it skyward. It soared up over the railing to clatter to the wooden platform. A bit of careful jostling finally knocked the spoon loose to tumble back down to me. I held up a hand to catch it, but nothing reached me.

The rope was too short. I'd done my best to weave as much as I could manage from the material I had on hand while still making it strong enough to hold me, but it hadn't been enough. The spoon twirled in the air several feet above my head. I chewed on my bottom lip as I looked for a solution. Five minutes of thinking and I'd only come up with one idea, but in truth it wasn't very promising. Still, it couldn't hurt to try.

I backed away from the wall, pulling the rope with me until the spoon had risen all the way back to the edge of the platform, then launched myself toward the arena wall. I sprinted forward, kicked off the wall, and leapt up into the air as I reached for the spoon. I missed.

My hand closed on empty air as I tumbled back to the ground in a heap. I pushed up onto my knees, spit out a mouthful of sand, and glared at the spoon that now lay on the ground beside me. I could just imagine the stupid little shit taunting my feeble efforts. I was two inches away from freedom, but it might as well have been two hundred miles.

I gauged the distance again as I stood to my feet, and I could see why I hadn't gotten high enough. I'd been thinking about the ground when I'd jumped, and thinking about landing again had sapped some of the strength from my legs. I was pretty sure that I could make it if I gave that jump everything I had and then some. Probably. Of course, if I missed again I was in for a much harder landing than the last one. I'd covered bigger distances when I'd leapt across Byzantia's rooftops, but it was easy to jump as hard as you could manage when the alternative was a broken neck. Still, risking a twisted ankle seemed like a better alternative than another round in the arena games.

I tossed the spoon back over the railing, took a few deep breaths, and threw myself forward. This time I used my momentum to take two good steps up the wall before I flung myself up and out. I spun around and reached out as I soared through the air, straining forward like a drowning man reaching for a life rope. My fingers brushed metal and grabbed hold.

The force of my swing carried me up and out over the sand. I tossed a dizzy glance down to the ground that spun beneath me as I began to fall backward, then scrambled up the rope and heaved myself up to grab the railing. The wood was slick with rain, but I held on tight and swung my other hand up to latch on as well. I hung there for a moment, dangling above the ground like an exhausted plum before harvest, then slowly began to pull myself up to safety.

"You could find easier exercise inside."

The voice came from just above my head. I looked up in shock to see a heart-shaped face, olive brown skin, and intense yellow eyes staring back into mine. I gasped as my grip slipped off the railing, and then I was falling.

My thoughts tumbled right along with me all the way to the ground as I tried to make sense of what had just happened. I hit the dirt before I had a good answer. The sand was softer that a cobbled street, but not by much. I bounced hard and landed in a tangle of limbs a few feet away. My vision danced with pops of color and swirls of black and I had to think really hard about breathing before my lungs finally remembered what to do. I coughed, the gasped, then forced myself to move.

Everything hurt, but at least it was the throbbing ache of deep bruises rather than the sharp stab of broken bones. I pushed myself up onto one elbow just in time to see a figure walking towards me through the rain.

It was the halfling woman I'd seen lurking in the shadows when I'd first arrived in the arena. She moved with the steady, deliberate grace of a cat hunting sparrows, and she carried a knife. Its blade was half the length of her leg and scattered stray shards of light off its razor edge as she moved. She stopped next to me and crouched down until her face was level with mine.

"Going somewhere?"

"I was until you showed up and scared a week's worth of shit out of me. What in the hells are you doing out here?"

"I would ask the same question of you."

I almost snapped back at her, but she had a knife and a hard look in her eye, so I decided to play it civil for as long as possible.

"I'm getting out of this death pit while I still can, and if you had half a brain in your skull you'd be coming with me instead of getting in my way."

What? I never said I was *good* at being civil.

"I think it is you who is missing their brain," she said with a shake of her head. "Unless you've found some way to deal with your effigy."

"My what?"

Then I remembered the strange little lecture Trebonious had given me as he dipped a lock of my hair in my own blood. He'd claimed he could use it to visit a nasty death upon me if I ever caused him trouble, or some such nonsense. I snorted a little spray of water from my nose.

"You don't actually believe that horseshit is real, do you?"

"I do, and it is. Did you not stop to wonder why it was so easy to leave in the first place?"

I'd noticed that very thing, in fact, but had just chalked it up to uncommon good luck. I had to admit that Farshore's arena was, without a doubt, the most poorly guarded prison I had ever seen. Almost as if they weren't terribly bothered by the idea of someone breaking out of it…

"If you run you will die."

She spoke the words with such casual certainty that for a moment I almost believed her. I'd been so busy trying to keep my skin in one piece that I'd forgotten all about the damned thing, so I hadn't bothered to factor it into my escape plans. Could that sour-faced little scarecrow really use a bloody chunk of hair to reach out and kill me?

Then I got a hold of myself. No doubt Trebonious was simply clever enough to use the locals' superstition against them by making them too scared to run for it. I gave him credit for a good con, but that didn't mean I had to fall for it too.

"Thanks, but I'll take my chances."

Sheska's knife was at my throat. I hadn't even seen her move, but suddenly her blade dug a painful line across my skin.

"You will not. If you insist on trying I will kill you myself."

I held very, very still. I'd seen bluffs before. This was not one of them.

"Why do you care? If you're right then Trebonious will kill me, if you're wrong then I get to enjoy my life in peace. What difference does my fate make to you?"

"None," she said with a shrug. I tried not to wince as her blade bit into my skin. "But if you go over that wall then the small man in black will reduce our rations to make an example. I am more fond of a full meal than I am of you. Now make your choice. I find this rain unpleasant."

For a moment I thought about flinging sand at her eyes and rolling away to make a run for it, but something told me that even a bit of dirty fighting wouldn't be enough to get the drop on her. The small woman gave me chills, and it wasn't just from the cold water that ran down the back of my shirt. I sighed and pushed her blade away.

"Fine, you win. Let's get back inside."

She nodded and watched me struggle to my feet without offering to help. Then she kept right on watching me, following a few steps behind as I hobbled my way across the sand, down the ramp, and back through the arena door. I pulled it shut behind us and dug out my makeshift picks to lock the door again.

"You know, if we worked together I think we could get our hands on the—"

She was gone by the time I turned around. I hadn't even heard the whisper of her boots on the stone floor, and that simple fact left me feeling far more nervous than even her wicked looking knife had managed. I thought about popping the door for a third time and making a break for it, but I couldn't shake the thought that she would know about it somehow, and probably wouldn't bother to stop and chat if I tried to scale the wall again.

I sighed and limped back to my cell. Planning my escape had kept me focused and effective, but I felt that sense of purpose drain out of me with each step. I stepped into my room, pulled the door shut, and flopped down on my cot without even bothering to peel off my soggy clothes. An hour ago I'd been riding high on thoughts of freedom. Now all I had was wet clothes, an aching back, and a future full of fighting and pain until the odds finally caught up with me and put me in the ground for good.

CHAPTER 8

"Damn it, Charity! Keep your guard up if you want to keep your head."

I bit back a stream of choice curses and crawled my way back onto my feet, ignoring the screams of protest from the muscles in my hips, thighs, shoulders, arms, and more as I bent to retrieve my wooden training swords and resumed a fighting stance in front of Cael.

The sad and sodden end to my hopes of escape had left me in one hell of a funk. I picked at my food, kept to myself, and snapped at Alleron when he'd asked what was bothering me even though he'd been the only one to notice or care enough to do so. A week went by without games being scheduled, and then another. I overheard two of the guards discussing the cotton harvest, so I gathered that a good portion of the city must have been too occupied with picking and bagging for it to have been worth scheduling new festivities. No point in forcing people to kill each other if no one bought tickets to come and watch.

As much as I'd come to dread seeing my name on the games' list again, a few weeks of drudgery were the last thing I needed just then. My sleep grew worse every night, and before long I felt worse than I can ever remember feeling without actually being sick or on the verge of starvation. I finally realized that I needed to find something to occupy myself with if I wanted to avoid going full on insane. Given that needlepoint wasn't an option, I eventually decided that if I couldn't escape another trip to the arena then I might as well spend my time improving my odds of surviving it.

It took me a full day to work up the courage to ask Cael for help, but to my surprise he'd been eager to do so. I thought he'd felt sorry for me. Turned out he was just a horrible sadist who enjoyed yelling at girls and whacking them on the head with a training sword whenever they let their guard slip. Bastard.

He'd been driving me harder than a Verangi slave master, and every time I paused or complained he just used the distraction to hit me again and tell me that I'd be dead right now if we'd been fighting for real.

After my first week of abuse I learned to save my breath for the training, and even though I'd fallen asleep cursing his name and thinking of exquisitely painful ways to kill him, I had to admit that Cael's methods were proving effective. I'd begun to notice the change in my body as my muscles hardened and absorbed his lessons, and some of the stances, parries, attacks, and evasions I had once thought impossible had begun to feel routine.

"Blood of the gods, are you swatting at flies? Stop waving those toothpicks around and perform the exchange like I've shown you."

Cael had started me out with a broadsword and shield, the proper weapons of a warrior, as he'd called them. He'd gone on and on about how a good shield provided both defense and offense in a trained warrior's hands. I gave it my best try seeing as the shield he'd given me had saved my life in the fight against the elementals, but I'd lacked the upper body strength to do much more than hide underneath it and wait for the beating to stop.

In the end it had been Alleron who'd suggested that I exchange both weapons for two sabers. Apparently it was a common fighting style among his people, who were lighter and shorter like me. The first time I'd fought with them had been a revelation. You don't have to be stronger than your opponent if you're fast enough to turn his guard with one blade and strike through it with the other. Cael had grumbled about it for days, but I'd taken to it immediately and refused to fight with anything else after that.

One evening over dinner I asked Alleron why he kept helping me out. I wasn't used to kindness that didn't come with a string attached or a dagger hidden inside it. He hadn't done anything to make me question his motives yet, and that was starting to make me very uncomfortable.

"Well, for one thing your unlikely win against Borus won me more beer and favors than I'll be able to enjoy in ten lifetimes, so I suppose I feel indebted to you."

"Wait, you wagered that I'd win?"

"Of course I did," he answered, seeming honestly confused by the question. I suppose I should have been flattered, but all I could think in the moment was that he'd just removed the last doubt I'd had as to whether or not he was completely crazy.

"In truth, however, I'm helping you because I have great hopes you'll do the same for me in the future."

Ah, now we were getting back into more familiar territory.

"Have anything specific in mind?" I asked cautiously.

"I do, indeed. Someday in the not too distant future you're going to help me save my people."

"Oh…is that all?"

I honestly didn't know how to respond to that. I would have assumed he was joking if his expression hadn't gone so serious all of a sudden.

"You sure you got the right Byzantian? Lot of girls with brown skin and black hair where I'm from."

"Quite certain. I had already seen your face many times before you arrived here."

Then a lopsided grin spread across his face like sun breaking through the clouds as he leaned back in his seat.

"Then again, perhaps my visions have finally pushed me over the edge and I don't even realize how mad I am. Who can say?"

I let out the breath I'd been holding and smiled back in relief as I shook my head at his poor joke. In truth, his words had sent a shiver through my gut, but I hid my unease beneath a laugh.

"I knew you were full of shit. Don't know how you'd expect me to save anyone from in here anyways."

"Oh, we won't remain in the arena much longer."

I sat up and looked around, suddenly nervous. Even with the noise in the dining hall his voice was pitched a tad too loud for comfort.

"Not so loud. You got a plan then?"

"Nothing like your little midnight escapade, if that's what you're asking."

"You know about that?"

He smirked and waggled his fingers at me.

"Wizard, remember? Diviner extraordinaire. I may be working off of old information without my equipment and reagents, but I knew you'd try to go over the wall. Would have stopped you myself if Sheska hadn't beaten me to it."

"Is that the halfing?" I asked with a scowl. He nodded.

"I still have half a mind to find a quiet moment to resume our little conversation when she isn't looking. I would have been ten miles gone by now if that *bruta* hadn't stopped me."

"More like six feet under the ground," he chuckled. "Your arena master may be just a human, but he's learned quickly. The effigies he crafted are no jest, and neither is Sheska, so I'd recommend you leave her be if you enjoy breathing and having all your limbs fixed in place."

"Really? She's the only one in here who's smaller than me."

"Indeed, and she also holds the record for most kills in the arena now that Borus is no more."

He laughed at the look of shock that settled onto my face.

"Halflings are rather…feral, you see. Most have the good sense to leave them be. 'A halfling never goes hungry,' as the old saying goes."

"What does eating have to do with it?"

"Quite a lot, given that halflings eat what they kill."

"Oh." I felt another one of those shivers Sheska had given me trace its way down my spine. Seemed that the stories of horrible man-eating mythics in Farshore weren't entirely false, they were just shorter than I'd expected.

"In any case, now that your abortive venture is behind us it should only be a matter of days before we're on our way."

"On our way to what, exactly?"

"Why spoil the surprise?"

"I hate surprises."

"In that case, Charity my dear, I suggest you prepare yourself for a long string of disappointments. Oh, do you plan on finishing that loaf?"

My cycle of training, eating, and sleeping continued on, folding over on itself until the routine was all I knew. I have no idea how long my days might have gone on like that, if it all hadn't changed one morning without warning.

***

I awoke to the sound of hammering, sawing, and the muffled shouts of men hard at work filtering down through my stone ceiling from the arena floor overhead. I'd become accustomed to waking in my own good time, so the intruding noise had me in a foul mood by the time I'd dressed and made my way down to the mess hall. It was more crowded than usual, nearly as full as the evening I'd first arrived.

Looks like I'm not the only one who got turned out of their bed early by all this racket.

I spotted Alleron at a nearby table, and noticed that he'd somehow managed to keep a seat open. I wove through the crowd and plopped myself down in it with a grunt.

"What in the eight frozen hells is going on up there?" I asked as he slid me a plate of eggs and roasted potatoes.

"Today is Farshore's seventieth year of glorious existence, don't you know? Seems that the occasion calls for something extra special for today's games."

"Are they building us a fleet to hold naval battles?"

The hammering and banging could be heard even above the din of conversation in the crowded room.

Alleron just shrugged, but pointed towards my plate of food.

"Better eat hearty, just in case."

It was sound advice, so I set about following it. As I scraped the last of the food off my plate, a voice from across the room shouted that the pairings for today's games had just been posted, and the room echoed with the scrape of dozens of benches and chairs on the stone floor as everyone stood at once to go look for themselves.

"It finally begins," Alleron whispered to himself. Or, at least I thought that's what I heard him say. With all the racket it was hard to be sure. When I turned to ask him what he was on about this time I realized that he was already halfway to the door, so I scrambled to catch up with him.

The training room was more crowded than I'd ever seen it, but we managed to press our way through. The familiar sheet of paper was nailed to the central post, but this one had only a single list of names on it instead of the usual two columns of paired names that designated that day's matches. I elbowed my way closer, and saw the words "Battle of the Victors" in large script across the top, followed by a very short list of names. Mine was among them. So was Alleron's. In fact, the eight names on the list were the winners of the last three games.

"So, what then?" I asked a gray-haired man standing next to me. "Today's games will only have one match? Some sort of battle to the death?" The thought of the carnage that would ensue if they set us against each other all at once turned my blood to ice, but I tried to keep my expression calm and disinterested.

"One match, aye, but Cael made the announcement when he posted the sheet. You won't be fighting against each other. You'll be fighting as a team."

At first I wasn't sure I'd heard him right, but I soon realized that it was all that anyone else was talking about. Alleron beamed at me like a child who'd just learned he'd be allowed to eat his fill of sweet buns, but I could only offer a weak smile in return. I was relieved to learn I wouldn't have to cross swords with him, but that relief didn't have much room to grow next to the question that was taking up most of my thoughts.

If they intend for us to all fight together as a team…what in the eight hells are we going up against?

CHAPTER 9

"If anyone so much as touches my axe I swear I'll make a winter coat from their hide!"

Magnus shoved his way past me to be the first one into the weapon room. He raced across the room with surprising speed given the length of his legs, and lifted a huge double-sided war axe down from a rack.

"There's my girl. Have they treated you well? No nicks or scratches on you?"

The rest of us filed into the room while Magnus continued to whisper to his weapon as he checked its edge for signs of wear. I retrieved a pair of curved sabers from the sword table as the others spread out through the room to equip themselves as they saw fit. No one seemed inclined to talk, but the tension in the air was so thick you could have cut it with…well, just about anything in the room, actually. None of the victors had ever faced one another in the arena, obviously, but more than a few had lost a friend to the other's blade, and none were the trusting sort by nature.

In addition to Magnus and Alleron, the orc Nataka and Sheska herself had also been on the list. The remaining three were comfortingly human. Olney was a legionary veteran with a touch of white in his hair and an eyepatch covering his left eye, while Keegan was a bear of a man sporting a scraggly black beard and biceps the size of dinner plates. The third was a man named Cassus, a lean fellow with black hair that fell to his shoulders and eyes that never seemed to stop checking the shadows.

"Any of you have some sense of what we'll be facing up there?" I asked. I doubted anyone had much to offer, but a girl can only listen to the clatter of armor and the rasp of whetstones over blades for so long.

"Not I." Keegan's voice was muffled by the chainmail shirt he was attempting to squeeze over his head and shoulders. "Though I'll wager...unf, that it'll be something special. Why go to all this, aargh... trouble, otherwise?" He finally managed to get the chainmail settled onto his torso. Didn't look like he could breathe too well, but he seemed pleased.

"Well, shouldn't we discuss some tactics, then?" I asked the room. "You know, compare strengths and weaknesses and such. We'll stand a better chance against whatever they have planned if we work together."

"I hunt alone," said a voice by my ear. It took all the self-control I could muster not to jump five feet in the air. Instead I turned around to find Sheska crouched on top of the table behind me, staring at me with her strange yellow eyes. She carried a shortbow and a quiver full of arrows, and had painted a pair of black soot lines across her face.

"If you get in my way, you are dead. If you do not, you may do as you please."

"Right, um, that's more or less what I was talking about, I suppose. Thanks."

Sheska nodded once, but didn't take her eyes off me. Even though she was less than half my size, I started to think that now I had a better sense of how a dormouse feels when a cat prowls into the room. I didn't want to be the first one to look away. No sense in letting her know how badly she unnerved me, so I squared my jaw and glared back at her. Just when I was starting to think that getting into a staring contest with a halfling might be a losing proposition, the arena master's voice thundered down the passageway.

"Fighters, to your stations!"

Sheska blinked once, sniffed, then jumped down from the table and walked past me towards the door. I turned to find Alleron trying to hide a smile as he shook his head. I shot a glare in his direction and joined the others in heading for the door.

We all walked up the ramp together, and I found myself feeling a good deal more confident than any of the other times I'd made the journey before. I still had no idea what we'd be facing once we got up there, but thanks to Cael and Alleron I was significantly better prepared to deal with whatever Trebonious threw at us. Besides, I was now surrounded by a pack of battle-tested fighters who had fought and won before. I figured all I really needed to do was focus on keeping myself alive and in one piece, and they could take care of the rest.

As we approached the top of the ramp I realized that it was later in the day than I'd thought. It was dark, but the arena floor was lit by hundreds of blazing torches that ringed the top of the wall.

"What in the bloody hells is all this?" Olney grumbled from the front.

I had to wait for the rest of the group to shuffle through the entrance before I could see what he was talking about. The arena floor had been transformed. It was filled with an artificial forest of wooden trees that stretched from wall to wall. A platform that had been made to resemble a rocky cliff face rose above them in the center, and a path led towards it from the ramp entrance.

Guess we know what was causing that racket all day. But why did they go to all this trouble?

One thing was certain; there was no way Trebonious had put all of this together just to throw us a celebration picnic. With the torchlight shining in my eyes I couldn't see the crowd in the stands, but I heard enough excited whispers and shuffling to know that every available seat was filled, though it seemed that for some reason they had been told to remain silent as we entered. What I could see in the shadows of the torchlight were dozens of men standing all along the top of the wall, each one holding a crossbow at the ready.

"My noble lords and dames, welcome to these special games," the arena master's voice echoed in the eerie silence.

"In the name of the Five Divines, and in honor of Farshore's seventieth glorious year, Governor Caligus bids you welcome! Tonight the finest champions ever to grace the arena sands will fight for your entertainment and the glory of the gods."

I looked around, but I still saw no sign of who they were expecting us to battle. Were other fighters hiding out there among the trees?

"Warriors! In the name of the Five Divines, fight with honor, die with courage, live on in glory. Begin!"

I'm not ashamed to admit that I jumped a bit when the heavy wooden doors of the passageway slammed closed behind us, but otherwise nothing moved as the echo faded away.

"Bah!" Keegan snorted in disgust as he frowned down at me, then turned and marched straight down the path that led towards the false cliff face at the center of the arena. I looked at Alleron, but he just shrugged and followed the others in Keegan's wake. The hairs on the back of my neck were prickling with unease, but I preferred staying with the group to hanging back on my own, so I hurried to catch up with them.

We drew closer to the platform, and I spotted a large opening towards the top. It looked like the entrance to a cave. As we stepped into the small clearing that surrounded the cliff, the squeal of rusty metal hinges echoed out of the cave. The sound cut off as abruptly as it had started, then a pair of orange eyes flared to life in the darkness.

More than ten thousand pairs of lungs drew in a startled gasp all at once as a shape emerged from the cave and began to climb down the platform. It looked a lot like a cat, but as it reached the ground and started stalking its way towards us I realized that it was easily twice the size of a horse. Its coat was as black as spilled ink, and it moved with the fluid grace of a hunter on the prowl.

"Kla ses ka'sani netak," I heard a shaking voice say beside me, and I looked down to see Sheska rooted in place, her eyes wide with shock and fear as she stared at the approaching monster. "Mother and Father save us, a Jauguai."

The huge creature crouched low to the ground, its tail lashing back and forth as its gaze darted to each one of us in turn.

"Keep your skirts on, little one," Keegan chuckled as he stepped forward. "It's a might bigger than most, but it's just a cat all the same. Should make a nice rug for my room." He clashed his sword against his shield as he rolled his shoulders and stepped forward.

"Come on, kitten. Let's see what you look like on the inside."

The beast snarled, and two black tendrils rose up from its shoulders to sway in the air above its head. They looked exactly like its tail, except that each was tipped in a curved, bone-white talon that looked wickedly sharp even from here.

"Well, that's different," Magnus muttered as he hefted his axe. He started to move towards Keegan, but Sheska grabbed his arm.

"Stop, you fool! Do not move. Do not even breathe."

"Let me go, you crazed she-devil," Magnus pulled his arm free.

"Raaaargh!" Keegan bellowed, and leaped forward.

The Jauguai roared in answer, a hungry, feral challenge that rattled my bones. Then it disappeared.

One moment the huge cat was standing there plain as porridge. The next its shape blurred and warped like smoke for an instant before it vanished completely. Keegan's charge turned into a stumbling halt.

"What in the eight frozen—"

The air in front of his face blurred black, then his head was torn from his shoulders. A crimson spray of blood shot into the air as his headless body stood motionless for a brief moment before it collapsed like a puppet whose strings had just been cut.

The crowd erupted in a chorus of shrieks and cheers. Before my brain had managed to wrap itself around what I'd just seen I heard a scream behind me, and spun around to see Olney kicking and flailing in the Jauguai's jaws. The beast crunched down hard and the flailing stopped. It dropped the limp body to the ground, licked the blood from its muzzle with a long, pink tongue, then disappeared again.

"Form up!" Nataka shouted. "Back to back. Now!"

Her gruff voice broke through my shock, and I jumped to take my place in the outward-facing circle we formed, my swords raised and ready. I scanned the open ground in front of me, starting at every flickering shadow cast by the torchlight, but saw nothing that would reveal the beast's presence.

"What in the bloody hells is that thing?" Cassus sounded even more terrified than I felt, which I hadn't thought was possible.

"Jauguai hunt the deep jungles of my home." Sheska stood beside me, an arrow drawn back on her bow and both eyes searching the trees. "I have never seen one before, but I know the stories. They are demons clothed in flesh."

"I could handle a demon if I could see it," Magnus grunted. "How does it keep disappearing like that?"

"He cloaks himself in shadow. We will not see him until it is too late."

"Then how do we kill it?" I asked.

"Kill it? Ha!" Sheska actually sounded amused. "You don't kill Jauguai. If they hunt you then you run, you hide, or you die."

"Not terribly fond of any of those options, personally," Alleron said behind me.

"Then why are we just standing out in the open waiting to be ripped to shreds?" Cassus' voice was laced with panic, and when I glanced back at him I saw that he was sweating like he'd just been jolted out of a nightmare.

"Because," I answered, careful to keep my voice calm and even, "if we stand together we can watch each other's backs. That's something, at least."

Another roar split the air from the trees in front of me, but when I spun around all I saw was the briefest hint of black gliding between the trees.

"No, no, no, no," Cassus stammered, "you sods can stand here and get eaten if you like, but I'm getting gone."

"Wait!" I shouted, but he was already racing down the path towards the closed doors of the ramp entrance.

He covered about half the distance in short order. Just when I started to think he might reach the doors one of the cat's strange shoulder-tails whipped out of the trees. The curved talon buried itself in his back, then pulled him off his feet to fly several feet backwards. Cassus landed in a heap, and had just enough time for one horrible scream before the Jauguai blurred back into view and ripped him to pieces. Once the beast had reduced the man to bloody shreds it turned to look back at us, and I swear by the gods that it grinned at me before it faded from view once more.

Panic screamed through me and set my limbs trembling. Our group was down by three in just about as many minutes, and I expected more would follow soon. I knew I needed to think clearly now more than I ever had before, but one thought kept repeating itself in my mind over and over, leaving no room for anything else.

This can't be happening, this can't be real. This can't be happening, this can't be real.

Since arriving in Farshore I'd bounced from one immediate problem to the next so quickly that I hadn't had time to stop and really absorb everything that had happened. Life had been hard back in Byzantia, but at least the rules made sense and I knew how to handle each day as it came. Now I stood back to back with an elf, a dwarf, an orc, and a halfling while an invisible demon cat tried to decide what order it wanted to eat us in. It was like a bad children's story, except it was all real, and in a few minutes more it was going to be the death of me.

There is no problem that knowledge and sound reason cannot solve. Mother Shanti's oft-repeated words broke through the terrified chatter in my mind, and I felt like I could hear the impatient tapping of her shoe as she frowned down at me. Suddenly, I was a foolish girl again, whining and complaining when the solution was right in front of my nose if I would just bother to slow down enough to see it.

Alright, you blight-faced old nag. What would you say if you were here, eh? Her dry voice resumed its droning in my memory.

Every problem is composed of constituent parts. Cause to effect, Charity. Always cause to effect. Follow the chain until you reach the root cause of the problem, and you will find your answer.

My mind was finally working again, and a sudden growl that rumbled through the air behind me whipped it into full gallop like a frightened horse.

So what's the root problem? Several hundred pounds of bloodthirsty muscles and teeth. Except that's not really the problem, is it? That beast is scary, but together we could probably bring it down if we could see it coming. As long as it keeps disappearing like that, we're as good as dead.

We needed a way to force it into the open. I thought of one. The only problem was that I hated it almost as much as I hated shaking in my boots while death prowled around just out of sight. The only way I could think to draw the big cat out would require us all to work together, and that meant I'd be trusting my life to a bunch of strangers who weren't even human. If they decided to use me as bait to save their own skins there'd be nothing I could do to stop them. I knew, because in that moment I would have done exactly that to any one of them if it would have gotten me out of the arena alive. Still, I didn't see any other options.

"Alright, you lot," I said aloud. "I'm personally feeling thoroughly sick of being hunted by something I can't see. Shall we do something about it?"

"You have some magic that can break its cloak?" Nataka asked, sounding like she was ready to kill me herself for holding out on them.

"Not magic, but a plan. Or, something like a plan, at least."

"Let's hear it then, girlie," Magnus snapped, "Anything is better than standing here with my head up my ass waiting to be gutted."

"Well, we can't fight it if we can't see it, but it will just stay invisible until we give it an opening."

Sheska snorted. "Your words sound familiar. Perhaps because I said them myself not long ago?"

I gritted my teeth, but continued. "But it's not always invisible. It reappears every time it attacks. Why? I think it's because it can't keep up that cloaking trick while it's chewing on something."

"Hmmm, you may be right at that," Alleron said. "An illusion like that requires a great deal of effort."

"Right, so if we can lure it into attacking when we're ready for it, we can all attack at once and bring it down."

"Perhaps," said Sheska, though she did not sound convinced. "But will the creature not simply vanish again when we strike back?"

"I might be able to help with that, actually," said Alleron. "I think I have a sense of how it's managing to disappear. If we can force it to reveal itself for more than a few seconds I think I can keep it that way. Probably."

"If you're wrong then my axe will split you open before the beastie gets to you," grumbled Magnus.

"Keep it visible? That's it?"

My heart sank into my stomach. My plan had pretty much boiled down to "lure the cat into attacking and keep it busy so that Alleron can melt it into a puddle." After all his ramblings about magic, I was hoping for something a little bit more… permanent.

"I thought you were a grand and glorious wizard? Can't you burn it to cinders or turn it to stone?"

"Oh yes, of course, why didn't I think of that?" Alleron snapped. "If you have scrolls detailing the spell you had in mind and a few quiet months for study and practice I'd be happy to oblige you. If you'd prefer something right now, however, then I'm afraid that 'visible' is the best I can do."

"If I can see it then I can root it in place and leave it vulnerable," Nataka offered.

"Oh aye, and Hilda can find out what color its brains are," Magnus said as he gave his axe a quick twirl, "but how do we draw it out?"

"We run."

Sheska spoke as though she were suggesting a summer picnic, but even though my mind followed the logic of her plan, my stomach threatened to rebel at the thought.

"This creature is a hunter. It will stalk and harass until we show weakness. The elf remains in the center while we four run in opposite directions. It will attack, and he will have his chance."

"But what about the one it picks as its next meal?" I asked over my shoulder.

"Would you rather stand here until the Deathstalker attacks on its own time?"

I hated to admit it, but she was right. So far the Jauguai had kept its distance from our little circle, but it was bound to grow restless sooner or later. Standing still was a death sentence in the end. At least if we acted first we'd have the element of surprise, and maybe some slight chance of surviving the night.

"Alright," I nodded. "So, do we count to three, or—"

"Yaaargh!" Magnus bellowed as he charged out into the night. "Come get some you flea-ridden hellspawn!"

"…just start running."

Sheska and Nataka were already racing in opposite directions. I drew in a deep breath, tried not to wonder if it was going to be my last, and began sprinting towards the fake trees in front of me.

Running is usually something I do very well, but that time my heartbeat was hammering in my ears before I'd taken ten steps, and my breath burned hot in my lungs. My eyes kept darting left, right, and up even though I knew they wouldn't see death coming for me anyway.

Every muscle in my back and shoulders was clenched tight as I waited to feel a set of razor-sharp claws tear into them at any moment. I'd been in a lot of bad scrapes before, but I had never felt as helpless and vulnerable as I did running exposed across the open ground, certain that two tons of hunting fury were watching my every step.

Then I saw it, a faint ripple in the air right in front of me like heat rising from a baker's oven on a cold day. Normally I doubt I would have even noticed it, but now my mind screamed a warning and I dove to the ground without a second thought. I felt a rush of wind as a heavy paw slashed through the air where my head had been a split second before. Then I hit the dirt and tucked into a ball. When I rolled to a stop I looked up to find the Jauguai staring right back at me.

Its head was enormous, nearly the size of one of the three-man tables in the arena pits. I was lying pinned between its two front legs, surprised to find I was still breathing. The big cat looked surprised too, but only for a moment. Then its glowing eyes narrowed to slits and its lips pulled back in a snarl that revealed a set of teeth the length of kitchen knives still stained with blood. It reared back and opened its jaws, and I knew I was about to die.

"Haaaiiii!" a shrill battle cry split the air, and a second later two arrows thudded into the Jauguai's neck. It reared back with a snarl of pain and surprise, giving me enough room to roll clear. I jumped to my feet and saw Sheska racing towards me with another arrow already drawn back, her small face alive with battle fury. Further behind her I saw that Alleron still stood where he'd been when I'd started running. It looked like he was just staring down at his hands and muttering to himself, and for a second I wondered if he'd lost his cool just like Cassus had.

As the Jauguai recovered from its shock, its form began to warp and blur once again.

"Now or never, Alleron!" I shouted. The elf looked up, and his eyes were glowing with an eerie green light.

He shouted out a string of strange words, and I felt a tingle ripple across my skin. Air pressed in against my ear drums like the feeling before a storm breaks loose, and then that same green light sprang to life around his hands. He flung them out with his fingers pointed at the Jauguai, and the light shot across the space between them to wrap itself around the huge cat just as it finished its vanishing act again.

The Jauguai was gone, it's massive black body invisible once again. But this time, a perfect green outline of its shape shimmered in the air. The glowing green cat shape turned and began moving towards the trees, and from the way it walked without turning towards us I knew that it didn't realize we could see it plain as day. For the first time since it had come stalking out of its cave I felt a surge of hope.

Nataka came running from my right. She twirled her spear above her head, but instead of using it to attack she skidded to a halt and slammed the butt into the earth.

"Legra and Sodek, Dwellers in the Deep Earth, wake your kin!" The Jauguai's head whipped around at the sound of her voice. It turned and crouched to leap at her, but a sudden rumble in the ground halted its attack. Then a tangle of thick roots burst up all around the cat and began to wrap themselves around its legs and body. The Jauguai howled and began to thrash in wild fury, but for every root it snapped three more whipped up around it. Soon it was bound tight to the earth.

"Your blood is mine, Deathstalker!" Sheska ran past me, an arrow aimed straight at the cat's eye. She was so focused on her target that she didn't see the Jauguai's shoulder-tails whipping towards her until it was too late. One talon buried itself in her shoulder while the other tail wrapped around her leg, and with a heave they flung her up off the ground. She arced through the air, and I realized that she was sailing straight towards the monster's open jaws.

Dammit to all the hells. I leaped towards the cat before I could think better of it.

The halfling wasn't a friend. In fact, she'd made it clear that she'd rather gut me than share a meal. But she had just saved my life less than ten heartbeats ago, and that was the kind of debt I didn't like to leave unpaid. I ran up a thick cable of roots, keeping my balance just like I would if I'd been moving along a rope line between rooftops back home, then jumped up to land on its shoulders and struck out with my sabers.

I grinned as my blades drew another howl from the beast, and its two shoulder-tails thudded to the ground. Sheska tumbled to a stop a few feet from the Jauguai's snapping jaws. She sat up, yanked the bone talon from her shoulder with a grunt, and stared up at me with a look of total shock.

"Drazi kan Kahad!" Magnus bellowed. His war cry echoed in the air as he leaped over Sheska where she lay sprawled on the ground and brought his axe down on the Jauguai's forehead. The thwack that it made as it hit home would have done a timberman proud. The beast roared and heaved itself at Magnus, but the roots held it fast. For a moment I thought that the cat's rage would somehow keep it fighting on even with an axe buried in its skull. Then the yellow light faded from the monster's eyes and it slumped to the ground.

My breath came fast and heavy as I jumped down from its back. I heard a roaring, whistling sound in my ears. For a moment I wondered if the strange magic they'd been throwing around had played havoc with my hearing, until I realized that what I heard was the frenzied cheering of the crowd in the arena stands.

"By all the gods! Truly we have witnessed a battle worthy of song and praise."

The arena master's voice thundered through the stands, bringing me back to reality. Despite his enthusiasm I sensed a note of true surprise in his words, and I guessed that none of us had been favored to survive the night. If we'd fought alone I had no doubt we'd each be lying in a pool of our own blood right now, but working together had turned out better than I'd dared hope.

"My lords and dames, I give you your champions!"

"Bah!" Magnus snorted as he yanked his axe out of the Jauguai's skull and slung it across his shoulder.

"Damned crazy human sacks of—" his voice trailed off as he turned and marched back towards the arena entrance.

Sheska was still staring at me, her face a mixture of confusion and murderous rage. It would have bothered me if I had enough energy left to worry about it. Now that the danger had passed all the adrenaline was quickly draining away from me. Suddenly I felt so tired that I started seriously considering a quick nap right there on the sand, and it left me in no mood for games.

"Problem?" I asked her.

The halfling opened her mouth, paused, then snapped it shut again and turned to follow after Magnus. I sighed and started making my own way towards the doors, not bothering to bow or salute the crowd. They could shower their empty praise on someone else, because just then the only reward I cared for was a bed and a good night's sleep.

CHAPTER 10

The walk down the ramp felt longer than it had before. The only sound I heard was the clatter of five pairs of boots on stone, three pairs fewer than the number that had walked up to the arena just a few minutes ago. I'd faced death before — the looming threat of starvation on the streets or the glint of a knife in a back alley — but I had always faced it alone, which meant there was no one but myself and the empty sky to see me walk away. I didn't know these people that walked with me back down into the pits, but we'd just stood together against a nightmare, and for a moment I'd felt like we'd been more than strangers.

I wished that I could think of something to say that could capture that feeling and make it real, but the only words that came to me sounded hollow and foolish. In the end I resigned myself to silence as we all returned our borrowed armor and weapons and made our way back into the pits. As we reached the branching point in the hallway, I squared my shoulders and turned to walk alone towards my room without looking back.

This is how the world is. How it will always be. No sense in crying over something you can't change.

The words sounded nice, but I still planned on indulging in a good round of sulking once I got back to my room. And that's probably exactly how I would have spent my evening if Cael hadn't been waiting for me outside my door.

When I first saw him I felt an unexpected thrill run down my spine. I had to admit that he was the kind of man that a girl looked at twice. He'd been far kinder to me than I'd had any right to expect, and my heart was still beating a little faster in my chest from the battle in the arena.

But when I saw the look on his face I gathered that he hadn't come for a social call. He seemed tense and distracted, and only acknowledged that he'd seen me with the briefest of nods as I walked up to him.

"Trebonious sent me to fetch you to his office," he said without greeting. I didn't need to hear the grim tone in his voice to know that this was not a good thing.

"Why? Or let me guess, he's angry that we survived that little death trap of his and wants to tell me what my horrible punishment will be in person?"

I didn't think he'd actually punish us for winning in the games. It seemed like a bad sort of precedent to set, but it was the only reason I could think of for why he'd have me brought to him now.

Cael just shook his head and started leading me back down the hallway towards the common room.

"No. If anything he seemed…excited."

You wouldn't think that would be cause for concern, but something in the way that Cael said it left me unsettled as we wove our way through the common room.

He nodded to the two guards stationed by the door. They lifted the bar and swung it open for us, and I found myself standing in the same stone hallway he had led me down when I'd first arrived at the arena in what now felt like a lifetime ago. Some stairs and a few turns later we approached the door to

Trebonious' office, and I saw that all four of my recent fighting companions were already waiting outside.

"What's this all about then, Cael?" Magnus grumbled. "I was just about to start in on my second pint."

"If I knew, Magnus, I still wouldn't tell you. Just hold tight until I return." Cael entered the office and closed the door behind him.

The others appeared relaxed, but I could sense that this unusual summons had them as much on edge as I was. Even Alleron seemed too caught up with his own thoughts for conversation, which was a first as far as I could recall. The only one of them to pay me any attention was Sheska. She studied me with that same focused glare she had been giving me ever since we killed the Jauguai, except this time there was no mistaking the anger that burned in her eyes. It had been a long day, and what little patience the Divines had given me had just about reached its breaking point.

"Look," I snapped, returning her glare and then some, "you've been eying me up and down ever since we walked out of the arena. If you've got something to say then let's hear it, otherwise find something else to stare at and leave me the hells alone."

The halfling blinked in surprise. Then she growled at me. I mean, she actually growled like a dog on a tether, which was not a sound I was used to hearing coming from someone who was more or less a person. For a moment I wondered if she planned on biting me, but with a visible effort of will she got a hold of herself and took a deep breath as though she was bracing herself for something unpleasant.

"You will have to take my life, human girl, for I will never be your slave."

"I'm sorry...what?"

"I will never be a slave again!" she shouted, her hands closing into fists.

Just when I thought I was starting to understand Farshore.

"Whoa, slow down," I said, raising my hands and trying to keep my voice calm and even. "Who said anything about making you a slave?"

She paused, and her anger slowly gave way to confusion as she realized that I truly didn't know what she was talking about.

"You saved my life, so now you hold my debt," she said, talking slowly as if she were explaining to a child that water is wet. "The Mother and Father's Law demands that now I serve you until the end of my days. They sent their servant to claim me, but you turned him back and stole me from their court. Death is my only escape from the curse you have placed on me. All I can do now is ask that you release me. Please."

The word caught in her throat a little, and I got the sense that this was the closest she had ever come to begging, which made me feel a little sick inside.

I guess the Divines aren't the only gods around who make unreasonable demands that ruin peoples' lives. At least this time I can do something about it.

"Look Sheska, all I know is that if you hadn't come charging in when you did I'd be enjoying a lovely view of the inside of a cat's stomach right now. You saved my life, I saved yours, and we both walked out of the arena on our own two feet. Can't we just shake hands and leave it at that?"

She startled back as if I'd just slapped her across the face, but she seemed more surprised than angry.

"You...you wish to declare Ko'koan?"

"Oh by Vesta's left ass cheek...sure, fine, why not?"

"Um, Charity..." Alleron whispered as he tugged at my sleeve, but I waved him off.

"If it will put all this to rest and keep you from throwing yourself off a bridge or cutting my throat while I sleep then I'll declare whatever the hells you want."

She studied me for a long moment, but just when I was starting to wonder if she'd dozed off or something her face lit up into one of the biggest grins I'd ever seen.

"Ha! You surprise me, young sister. In my wildest dreams I could never have imagined it, but your words feel right to me. We are both outcasts, both survivors, and you've proven your strength twice over. Stars know I would prefer a bondmate to a master…very well, from today we two will breathe as one."

"Uh…we will?"

I turned to find Alleron doing everything he could not to burst out laughing, and only partially succeeding.

"She doesn't mean that literally, right?"

After all the crazy magical things I'd seen since I got here that seemed like a question worth asking.

"Well, not literally, but close enough to count. In her tongue "Ko'koan" means "two who breathe as one." It's just about the strongest pledge the halflings make. Ko'koan share everything together. Food, danger…mates."

Sheska's grin grew even broader, which I hadn't thought possible.

"Now wait a minute, I didn't…"

The office door swung open. "The Master is ready for you now," Cael said as he waved us inside.

"Come sister," Sheska slapped my leg as she marched past me, "let's see what the pale human wants with us."

"Oh, this is too wonderful." Alleron still chuckled to himself as he followed after her. "I just love a good surprise, don't you? In my line of work they're far too rare."

"But I..."

"Move it, girly, you're blocking the door," Magnus said as he prodded my back. "If we hurry we might get through this damned interruption before those vultures pick the kitchens clean."

"No doubt the others give thanks to the spirits even now for the chance to eat a decent meal in peace, barrel belly," Nataka said under her breath as she stepped around us both to walk through the door.

"What's that, greyskin? It sounded like you were asking me what it feels like to be punched in the face by a dwarf."

By this time I was standing alone in the hallway, trying to make sense out of what had just happened.

"Are you just going to stand there?" Cael asked as he gestured for me to follow the others. I decided that sorting out the implications of whatever Sheska thought I'd just agreed to would have to wait, and stepped inside to find out what Trebonious had summoned us for in the first place.

The office hadn't changed since I stood in it last. Same shelves, same furniture, same table covered with strange items. Even the logs in the fireplace looked like the ones that had burned there before. Trebonious sat behind his desk, but he smiled and stood to his feet as I entered.

"And here is the young warrior queen herself, fresh from victory. I confess when you first came to us I didn't hold out much hope for your chances in the arena, but you've certainly proven me wrong on that account."

I heard the edge of frustration underneath his pleasant tone. No doubt I'd caused him a fair bit of grief and a great deal of lost coin when I'd beaten the odds and survived his death matches. I nodded to him in response but decided to hold my tongue until I had a better sense of his intentions. It turns out I actually can learn a thing or two eventually.

"In fact," he continued, "you've all shown yourselves to be quite formidable, not just individually, but as a team. Your victory over my little jungle curiosity was most impressive. Enough so that I've decided to extend a rare and generous offer to you."

"You could start with some decent blankets," Nataka interrupted. "Winter is coming and I'd rather not freeze to death in my cell."

Trebonious clearly did not enjoy being interrupted, but he managed to keep a thin smile on his face.

"I was thinking of something rather more substantial than linens."

"Such as?"

"Your freedom, for a start. Oh, and a great deal of gold as well."

No one spoke, but I could see that the others were just as surprised as I was, and just as eager to hear more.

"Ah, now I have your attention," Trebonious said as he reclaimed his seat and leaned back in his chair. "It is within my power as Master of the Arena to grant you each a full pardon, and I'm prepared to send you on your way with enough coin in hand to set yourselves up quite comfortably here in the city, or travel onwards to wherever you like."

"And I assume you want something from us in exchange, yes?" I asked. His offer was the stuff of dreams and children's stories, but even though I'd come to accept that life in Farshore involved a good deal more of both than I'd ever thought possible, I still recognized a baited hook when I saw one.

"Of course," he answered, "but nothing beyond your capabilities, as you've so recently demonstrated. I simply require that you retrieve something for me."

"And what would that be?"

"High King Tyrial's crown."

From the startled gasps and stunned looks you'd think he'd just asked us to raid the emperor's treasure vaults and kidnap his twin daughters. Even Cael looked surprised. In fact, Alleron and I seemed to be the only ones not showing much of a reaction, although in his case I suspected it was because he already knew what Trebonious would ask of us.

"Let's pretend that I only stepped off a ship from Byzantia a few weeks ago," I said, trying to keep the irritation I felt from creeping into my voice. I hated being the only one in the room who didn't know what was going on. Everyone turned to Alleron, clearly waiting for him to speak first.

"Tyrial was the last High King of the Elves." Alleron turned towards me with the same "looks like someone needs a history lesson" expression that Mother Shanti used to get right before she launched into a discourse on Grand Empress Jupricia's bowel movements or some such.

"It's been a long day, Alleron," I held up a hand before he could get started. "Any chance we could stick to the high points and save the details for later?"

"You want the high points?" Magnus grumbled. "How's this: the good king Tyrial managed to shove his head even further up his own ass than the rest of his elven kin. So much further, in fact, that he unleashed the greatest magical catastrophe Danan has ever seen on the rest of us."

I raised an eyebrow at Alleron, but he just shrugged.

"Our grizzled friend is correct, more or less. A little over five hundred years ago my people ruled all of Danan from our capital of Shirael Toris, the Shining City. Apparently Tyrial felt that death was an indignity he had no wish to suffer, and his search for alternatives seemed to have…gone wrong, somehow."

"Gone wrong?" Nataka scoffed. "That's a gentle way to speak of the Sundering. A decade of skyfire and drought, my people left homeless, your glorious city cursed for all eternity, and you call that 'gone wrong'?"

"I'm sorry," Alleron said through a thin smile, "I should have said that it seemed to have gone *very* wrong, somehow. The point is, the elves never truly recovered, and the western half of the continent is still a barren wasteland. Shirael Toris and everyone who lived there was destroyed in an instant, including Tyrial and his court."

"Which means you'll be spared a long and tedious search, as we know precisely where his crown can be found," Trebonious said from behind his desk.

"Are you mad, or just slow in the head?" Sheska asked. "Even in my jungles we know of the Shattered City. Anyone foolish enough to go within ten leagues of it is never seen again."

"Which is why I have waited so long to find such talented individuals as yourselves. I'm certain you'll have no trouble overcoming whatever minor difficulties might arise."

"Not bloody likely," said Magnus. "I'd sooner wrestle a hundred of your devil kittens than walk up to the gates of the Shattered City and knock. I fear no flesh and blood, but only a fool disturbs the restless dead."

"You can refuse, of course, and choose to remain here. I would be disappointed, but rest assured that would in no way affect your treatment here in the arena. I would redouble my efforts to present you with only the most glorious and challenging of contests to test yourselves against. I am certain you would all prove equal to the task."

I exchanged wary glances with the others, and saw that we all understood exactly what Trebonious was trying so hard not to say. If we refused he'd make sure we bled out in the arena within the week, and there wasn't a damned thing we could do about it.

"Let's assume for a moment that we do as you ask," I said. "What guarantee do we have that you'd hold to your end of the bargain?"

"I am both hurt and offended that you misjudge my character so badly, but as it so happens I suspected that you might require proof of my good intentions."

He opened a drawer in his desk, pulled out a small stack of papers, and spread them out in front of us. There were five of them, each with an intricate wax seal affixed to the bottom.

"These are your official pardons, signed and sealed," he said, tapping each one in turn. "When you return with the crown you can watch me dispatch them to the governor's villa yourselves, and Cael will join you on your mission to lend his aid and ensure that you remain focused on your task."

I snuck a sideways glance in Cael's direction. He looked surprised, but didn't offer any protest, which left me wondering what kind of hold Trebonious had over him.

"In addition, I have placed two hundred gold drachins on deposit at the Farshore Exchange in each of your names, which will await your successful return."

My mouth went dry. Ten drachins would keep a family fed for a year, and fifty would buy you a house on the banks of the Oxius.

As my brain struggled to wrap itself around the thought of me walking out of the exchange richer than a silk merchant, Trebonious opened a second drawer and withdrew a small wooden box.

"But just in case any of you might consider taking advantage of my generosity by escaping before retrieving the crown, I thought it only fair to remind you of the consequences that would entail."

He opened the box and removed its contents; five small loops of hair bound by silver thread, their ends crusted with dried blood. As he placed one on each of the pardons, I spotted my own curl of black hair among the red, brown, and golden blonde. Looking at it for just a few seconds sent a cramp through my gut and a shiver down my spine at the same time, and I could see that the others felt equally uncomfortable about theirs.

"I believe two months should be more than enough time for you to make the trip and return with the crown. Should you fail to do so within that time I would be forced to assume that you have broken faith with me, and that would leave me most displeased."

"So let me get this straight," I said, careful to look at Trebonious instead of my effigy. "You want us to march across the continent, find a lost city filled with unknown danger that will probably kill us, and retrieve a crown. If we say no, we're as good as dead. If we take longer than two months, we're dead for sure. But, if we somehow survive all of that and come back in one piece we'll gain our freedom and enough gold to keep Magnus swimming in ale until the day he dies?"

"You have a remarkable gift for summary, miss Charity," Trebonious said as he leaned back in his chair once more and awaited our answers.

I turned and looked at Alleron, Cael, Magnus, Nataka, and Sheska in turn. Each one gave me a grim but determined nod. I tried not to smile as I kept a lid on the surge of hope that flooded through me. I had just found my way home. I didn't like the sound of this Shattered City, but how bad could it be with a band of some of the toughest customers I'd ever met along for the ride? All I had to do was sit back, let them do most of the heavy lifting, and make my way back here in one piece to claim my freedom and more gold that I'd ever seen in one place. For a moment I could almost hear Byzantia's bells calling the hour and smell frying *kafta* on market day.

I turned back to Trebonious and added my own nod to theirs.

"Excellent!" he said as he stood to his feet. "I have horses and provisions standing by. You ride tonight, and may the Divines themselves attend your journey."

THE END

Want To Spend More Time With Charity?

GET SHADOWS OF THE PAST FOR FREE!

An orphan from the worst slum in Byzantia, Charity survived by running fast, thinking faster, and never letting anyone get too close. Being taken in by a sect of priestess-scholars was the kind of luck that urchins like Charity only dreamt of, but an unexpected letter from the last living soul she'd ever called friend forces her to break their rules and risk losing the only home she's ever known. Winding up back on the street would be bad enough, but when her night goes from bad to worse she'll be lucky to survive at all.

Just point your browser to

http://www.justinfike.com/shadows-of-the-past-download

Charity's adventure continues in

INTO THE SHATTERED CITY

If you enjoy this preview of Chapter 1 the full book is available now on Amazon.com

CHAPTER 1

Have you ever awoken next to a snoring dwarf with rocks and pine cones digging into your back and frost clinging to your eyelashes? Ridden a horse for so long your ass blisters and your legs go numb, then wake up before the sun rises to do it again? Lived on nothing but dry biscuits and cold water for weeks on end? If you answered no to any of the above, then count yourself blessed and lie, kill, or do whatever you have to do to keep it that way.

Our strange little group had been traveling westward for the better part of a week, and I'd been in a foul mood for most of that time. Alleron, Magnus,

Nataka, and Sheska all seemed thrilled to no end to be outside Farshore's walls. Alleron wouldn't shut up about how good it was to smell trees and clean air again, while Magnus kept disappearing into the woods and returning with some prized mushroom or strange moss for that night's stew.

Nataka maintained a running conversation of whispered muttering with herself. At first I thought the sun had baked her brains to mush, but when I asked if she was alright she said she was "speaking with the spirits of the land," which is how I learned never to ask an orc why she is muttering to herself. I even caught Sheska smiling once. A genuine smile of happiness, mind you, not the "I'm thinking of many ways to kill you" smile she usually put on.

Cael was the only one out of the whole lot who didn't seemed thrilled to be on this little adventure, and if I hadn't already respected the man then the frown he'd worn under his mustache since Farshore's flags and rooftops had disappeared beneath the tree line would have done the trick. It's not that I have anything against nature, per say. I'm glad that trees, thorny bushes, screeching birds and all the rest exist, and I'm perfectly happy to leave them all the hells alone if they return the favor. But there's a reason our ancestors invented lanterns, blankets, fireplaces, regular meals, and buildings with roofs and thick walls. Anyone who actually enjoys leaving all that behind to sleep on the cold ground and wear themselves out swatting at a never-ending swarm of bugs has more things wrong with them than Vesta herself would know how to cure.

My only comfort lay in the fact that Alleron had announced as we made camp last night that after more than a month on the road we were only about one more day's ride from the mountains that surrounded the Shattered City. One more day of discomfort and we would arrive at the object of our long journey, although that thought raised an entirely new set of concerns as I tried to roll out from under my blanket without slicing my face on the blade of the axe that Magnus insisted on sleeping with. He'd flatly refused to leave town at all until Trebonious sent someone to fetch "Hilda" from the arena armory, and he hadn't let the thing out of his sight since.

Most of the others were sleeping soundly, although I couldn't tell you how they managed that given the circumstances. We'd camped in the lee of a large grove of fir trees that provided a small measure of shelter from the biting wind, but if there was more than three inches of ground free of knobby roots and pine cones then I hadn't been able to find it. Sheska's bedroll was the only one empty, but she was always slipping away on her own business, so I didn't think much of it.

I trekked away from our little camp in search of a tree large enough to afford me some morning privacy, and tried to get my head around everything that had happened in the past month. The strange thing that my life had become still stole my breath away sometimes. Riding alongside an elf, a dwarf, an orc, and a halfling had become normal enough that I no longer jumped when I caught sight of one of them out of the corner of my eye, and the land we rode through was enough like the hills and forests outside Byzantia that you could be forgiven for thinking that the countryside was normal too. But it wasn't.

We rode through the heart of Danan, a land filled with mythic races, strange magic, and countless other storybook wonders. If someone had walked up to me on Byzantia's streets and started telling me about half of the things I'd seen since I stepped off the prison ship I would have run the other way to keep from catching whatever sickness had rotted their brain.

Not anymore. We'd fought things that writhed in the shadows of our campfire, stumbled into a field of flowers that moved about on their own and tried to put us to sleep with clouds of yellow pollen, and ridden three days out of our way to avoid a magical storm of chaotic energy that Alleron casually remarked would polymorph the lot of us into rocks and trees if we entered it. After the first week I stopped asking questions and learned to look three times before I went into the woods to take a shit.

And it wasn't just the dangers of the wilderness. We'd spent several days riding through boggy marshland to avoid an elven city. I'd been all for stopping in the moment I heard of it, but Alleron assured me that our strange band would not be well received by the city's patrols. As we traveled Nataka told me of her people's huge roving caravans on the western plains, Sheska spoke of massive stone cities in the heart of the southern jungles, and Magnus spun stories of dwarven holds on the outer island that rang with ale song and the signal horns of departing longships.

The picture of a land rich in history, conflict, and mistrust began to take shape in my mind even though I saw little more than its wild and untamed reaches as we traveled. I soon realized that Farshore colony was a just a small and lonely outpost of humanity on the coast of a continent far larger than the lands Byzantia claimed as its empire, and possibly even those of the nations beyond its borders as well. Danan was enormous, untamed, and strange in more ways than I could count. The more I saw of it, the more determined I became to make my way back home again, assuming we survived this little adventure and made it back to Farshore to claim our promised reward.

I'd long since made my peace with the fact that many things I'd grown up believing were nothing more than fable were actually all too real. Some part of me kept expecting to wake up from the strangest dream I'd ever had and swear off late-night drinking for good. But even though they hardly noticed any of the dozens of unusual sights that had left me speechless on our journey, I could tell from the looks my companions shared when we spoke of it that this Shattered City we rode towards was dangerous. They hadn't seemed particularly impressed by any of the dangers we'd overcome so far, so I could only imagine what kind of trouble lay ahead.

"I've caught us breakfast."

I jumped half way out of my skin, and only managed to avoid soiling my pant legs through some very deft footwork. When I regained my balance and turned around I found Sheska perched on one of the lower limbs of the tree with her shortbow in one hand and an impressively plump rabbit in the other.

"*Chaso di bruta*! You just frightened ten years off of me."

"You are not happy? After all your complaining over trail rations, I thought you would be pleased to eat fresh meat." She looked hurt, and I realized she'd gotten up early to go hunting for my sake.

"Of course I am, and thank you. But maybe cough or snap a twig or two the next time you sneak up behind someone who's not wearing pants."

She stared down at me for a moment, sniffed, and disappeared into the trees in the direction of our camp without saying a word. I sighed, finished cleaning up, and followed after her. Of all the strange new things in my life that I was having trouble adjusting to, "playing well with others" was at the top of the list.

By the time I made it back to camp Magnus already had the rabbit sizzling on a spit over a crackling fire. Within the first few days of our journey I'd discovered to my surprise that the otherwise taciturn dwarf warrior hid a deep love of cooking within his oak-barrel chest. So far it had been the only subject that he'd been willing to give more than a grunt or a few short words to.

"I stuffed this beauty with those grangia roots I dug up yesterday, plus a few sprigs of green onion and wild parsley. In a few minutes you'll think you're dining in King Olenson's own mead hall."

"Shouldn't we start breaking camp?" Cael huffed. "I'd prefer to be on the move before high noon."

"Aye, you most certainly should, longshanks. And while you're about it I'll get breakfast roasted and ready. Might even give you some, if you quit pestering me."

True to his word, Magnus had divvied up the meal before we'd packed away our things, and the wonderful smell easily banished any lingering complaints that might have been offered.

We gathered around the last embers of his cooking fire as he doled out a portion to each of us. I made a point of thanking Sheska again for providing our first decent meal all week, but she just shrugged my words away, and was still sulking by the time we broke camp.

We rode for the better part of the day without a rest. I would have given anything to get down off of that infernal torture device that everyone kept calling a horse, but I didn't want to be the first one to suggest it once again. Instead I just gritted my teeth and tried to keep up. I'd named my horse Shanti, because just like the good Vestan Mother she really was a horrible nag. She would wander off the trail to graze or wet the ground the instant I let the reins fall slack. I couldn't decide whether the aching in my back and arms or the bruises on my ass bothered me more. Still, I kept her mostly in line behind the others, and since no one else had the good sense to suggest a break, we made rather good time throughout the day. By the time the sun had begun to droop down into our eyes along the far horizon even I could see how the land had changed since we'd started out that morning.

For most of our journey we'd ridden through thick forests and open fields, forded rivers and skirted around lakes so large you couldn't see the shore on the far side. Now the endless wall of green trees had given way to sparse pine and outcroppings of jagged gray stone as we rode along a gravely ridge that wound up into the mountains. The trip had taken the better part of five weeks, more than half of the total time that Trebonious had named before he'd use the effigies he'd created to pull our guts out through our noses or something equally unpleasant. The others didn't seem concerned about it, though. Cael had said a few nights back that most of our time had been spent in charting a course through unfamiliar terrain. If we followed the same route back we could return in far less time.

Our horses had slowed to a crawl as we made our way up a particularly steep hillside, threading our way between a rocky cliff face that rose a good thirty feet overhead to our left, and boulders larger than a senator's carriage that lay strewn and jumbled down the slope to our right. The land rose steadily skyward in front of us, stretching up towards the blue sky overhead. We hadn't truly reached the mountains yet, but I could see that we were drawing close.

The sharp-witted among you will have realized by now that I was no great lover of the wild outdoors. Before coming to Farshore I'd only stepped outside Byzantia's walls a handful of times to assist Sister Hazera in gathering herbs. I didn't understand the sounds and rhythms of nature, so if you'd asked me at the time why the hairs on my neck had begun to prickle as my instincts started screaming at me to find a safe place to hide, I couldn't have told you why.

I didn't actually notice that all the birdsong had suddenly died away, leaving only an eerie stillness in its wake. I didn't notice that the logs and boulders that blocked our narrow path up ahead had no natural reason to fall where they were. All I knew was that every one of my senses was warning me of danger.

Most folk have felt that creeping sensation before, but most folk ignore it because they're stupid, and because the few among them who'd learned the hard way that they ought to trust their instincts had already bled out in a gutter somewhere before they could pass on the lesson. But if my life so far had taught me anything it was that whenever you feel like someone is watching you from the shadows with ill intent, it's usually because they are. Better to do something and look foolish that keep quiet and die brave and stupid.

"Um, guys, I think something's wro—"

Something buzzed out of the shadows to my left before I could finish my sentence. I threw myself against my horses' neck on instinct, and the arrow shattered against the rock where my head had been just a moment before. Shrill, screaming voices filled the air as hundreds of little grey-green creatures carrying clubs, spears, bows, and rusted short swords swarmed over the rocks all around us.

"Scratch that, something is *definitely* wrong!"

"Grodin ak'atz!" Nataka snarled. "Filthy goblin spawn."

Our group scattered as everyone leapt into action on their own. Magnus snatched Hilda from his saddle and flung himself off of his horse and straight at the nearest group of goblins while Nataka spurred her horse and charged in the opposite direction with her spear leveled. Cael had the presence of mind to throw his horse's reins over a tree branch before hefting his shield and broadsword, and I'd already lost sight of Sheska. Within the space of a few quick breaths Alleron and I were the only ones still sitting on our horses on the narrow trail.

Alleron shouted a string of syllables as a cascade of colored lights burst from his finger tips to leave a gang of screaming goblins stumbling and tripping blindly, but his spell managed to spook his horse at the same time. The beast reared back, dumping the wizard in a heap on the ground before bolting back down the trail the way we'd come. I drew the twin sabers that hung at my belt, but paused a moment to survey the scene rather than charging off in some random direction to start using them.

Everything was utter chaos. It looked like the goblins hadn't expected such a swift and fierce response, but they rallied and pressed forward in a never ending wave of tiny little bodies with murder shining in their beady eyes. Even the tallest among them would have barely reached my waist. Their heads, hands, feet, and ears all seemed too large for their bodies.

If it had only been a few of them attacking us I would probably have just laughed as they scrambled down from the rocks and waved their tiny weapons above their heads. Given that there were several hundred of them, the only thing I was interested in doing was getting the hells out of there with my skin in one piece. As the goblin horde closed in on us I had to admit that the odds of that happening were dropping by the second.

About The Author

I've loved stories for as long as I can remember. As a boy my grandma often told me tales of her adventures growing up on the South Dakota prairie as I drifted off to sleep, or filled my head with faerie queens, questing knights, and everything in between. Those stories shaped the way I saw the world and helped me understand my place in it. Eventually, I realized that I wanted to spin stories that would be just as important for someone else someday.

Pursuing that dream led me into a lifelong pursuit of the writer's craft, both on my own and by learning from some of the most well-regarded professionals in their spheres at the Masters in Creative Writing program at Oxford University.

I grew up in the Blue Ridge mountains of Virginia and was blessed to have a mother who didn't complain when I came home from the woods covered in mud and burs, and a father who told me the stories that sent him out there in the first place.

I live in Colorado with my amazing wife Mindy and pixie in disguise who permits me to claim her as my daughter at parties.

You can connect with me through my website:
www.justinfike.com
Or through my Facebook page:
www.facebook.com/JustinFikeAuthor/

Printed in Great Britain
by Amazon